T0156839

Straw Dreams

gloria cohen

iUniverse, Inc.
New York   Bloomington

Straw Dreams

Copyright © 2010 gloria cohen

This is a work of fiction. All of the characters, names, incidents,
organizations, and dialogue in this novel are either the products
of the author's imagination or are used fictitiously.

iUniverse books may be ordered through booksellers or by contacting:

iUniverse
1663 Liberty Drive
Bloomington, IN 47403
www.iuniverse.com
1-800-Authors (1-800-288-4677)

ISBN: 978-1-4502-4178-6 (pbk)
ISBN: 978-1-4502-4179-3 (ebk)

Printed in the United States of America

iUniverse rev. date: 9/29/2010

Acknowledgments

I would like to thank Caroline Nordquist, Lois Lewis, and my cousins, Gail Allen Rubinstein, Jennifer Futernick, and Joseph Baldino, for their invaluable aid. I want to give my grateful appreciation to George Nedeff, who was always there with his encouragement and confidence in me, as well as his time and help in the practical aspects of this project. And let me never forget and always be grateful to my friends who lovingly listen to my ideas and hopes with support, understanding, and very helpful feedback.

This book is dedicated to my brother
Harris Cohen (1936–1991).

Chapter 1

"I SHOULD HAVE WOKEN UP IN HELL." Softly, tonelessly, the words were expelled from the almost motionless figure on the bed.

"This isn't exactly heaven," answered the surgical resident as he sutured a ruptured tendon on the speaker's mutilated wrist.

True enough, she thought as she turned her head and looked at her surroundings. *Sterile-looking, austere,* were her first thoughts. Everything blended into a pale shade of green, including the curtain that shielded her from prying eyes. The bright, crisp white linen contrasted sharply with the steel grey of the instrument tray and the vessels on it, but then it all blurred and became a part of the dull, grey-green void that surrounded her. Now and then, something might clink against the metal table or its contents, or she might hear leather soles on the tile floor, but there was little else to break the sober silence. Sometimes she could hear muffled voices, but far in the distance, it seemed. Diane turned her head and looked at the doctor's face, his head slightly bent, as he concentrated on the gaping wound on her wrist. His pale face, framed by his bright red hair, was glaringly intrusive, made more so by his pointed red beard.

"This isn't exactly heaven," he had said.

And you, good doctor, bear a striking resemblance to some devil I've dreamed up, she thought sardonically. She examined his meticulously

1

trimmed beard, noticing the way it gained fullness at the jaw and then came to that careful point at his chin. His eyes were sharp and bright, but lurking within was his contempt for her misguided deed, she thought with certainty.

The devil would have given me a deep, hearty laugh, but you are most professional. Your very detachment seems a condemnation. She turned her head away and looked up into the large bulb above the bed, staring at the glaring rays emitted from the light. The brightness seemed to envelop her the way the defeat did. Failure had its own aura, mocking silently, but visibly proclaiming its dominance. It wouldn't be willed away; it wouldn't be stilled. The mechanism of the act, dreaded but anticipated, had been miserably ineffective. The knowledge burned her wrists; its ferocity left her limp. The silver blade came into focus again, held now in her left hand and hastily brought to the right wrist, brutally cutting into her pale and thin flesh, thoughtlessly spilling the blood out of its delicate and transparent vessel. Then a quick switch of the blade and the ritual repeated. Slash again because the blood is coagulating, the flow has stopped though the tub is covered with the stuff. Gleams of silver and slashes of red—stark whiteness of porcelain spattered with vermillion streaks. The fright was gone then, her numbing fear sucked into submission by a determined will.

"Now, turn your head. We're going to do the same thing to the other wrist," said the nurse.

She removed the long board from under the patient's back and arm and placed it at the other side of the bed. With her still-unsutured arm, the patient, now pale and wan, moved the pillow and took her position. She looked again at her outstretched arm. The blood had hardened, but it still had the bright red look she remembered; but when, how long ago had this happened? A needle was advancing toward her wrist; she turned her head. The overhead light claimed her eyes again; its rays engulfed her, wordlessly bidding her to obliterate the room and the world.

She barely felt the needle, the pressure of the thrust. Her eyes began to shut; a thick heaviness filled her mind, closing her to sensation. Her body was an object disowned, willed away and placed in competent hands. All that was left was her head, weighted and dark on the pillow.

A sharp prick on her wrist brought her back. It drew her mind into the present and focused her pain and her consciousness on her throbbing hand and the prickly sensation of a needle piercing flesh and pulling through. Winding and twisting, it hemmed and closed, securing skin and sinew, wiping away traces of red, visualization of fear. It was a wish almost realized but for a final thrust, its manifestation to be left in the wide lines on the pale wrists.

"Is she ready?" asked an attendant in a white tunic shirt.

"She's finished," replied the beneficent Mephisto rising from his seat after bandaging her arms.

The nurse moved the instrument tray aside and helped Diane to a sitting position. She stared at her wrists encased in the white gauze, her thin fingers protruding strangely through the splints. The nurse tied a sling around the right arm, more seriously injured than the left one, and instructed her to keep the arm elevated using a pillow at night.

Lethargically, Diane moved off the bed. The man in the white tunic waited ominously in the doorway. She advanced into the corridor, the waiting man joining her. A policeman, leaning against the reception counter, came toward her. She was abruptly prodded into a more wakeful state, roused from the apathy of her failure and her submission to caring hands. A sense of danger was implicit in the presence of these men. Warily she looked at her stalkers, fearful of continuing ahead yet aware that there was no alternative.

She looked tired. Her hair was uncombed, and a bit wild. The little lipstick applied hours ago had worn off, and her pale skin was without luster. She clutched her bag, a sweater dangling on top of the bag and between her hands. Her wrinkled clothes further added to an unkempt and disheveled, even disoriented look. *Why were they looking at her, almost leering at her,* she thought?

As though to compound her confusion, a doctor came up to her and in an almost friendly manner explained the procedure that would follow.

"I'm sorry, but we don't have a resident psychiatrist on our staff. We're going to take you to Metropolitan Hospital."

"I don't want to see a psychiatrist. I'm going home."

"I'm afraid we can't let you do that."

She fastened her eyes on the young doctor and said, "I'm perfectly rational and capable of caring for myself." She began to walk out of the reception area, her two bandaged arms still cradling her possessions, her legs taking what she thought were confident strides. But she was weary and her movements were slow and deliberate.

They wouldn't dare come after me, she thought. *They wouldn't try to physically restrain me; it was just a ruse.* But the policeman followed, softly entreating her to come along quietly. "I know you don't want to make a scene," he said softly, a clear warning in the words. The threat hit its mark. They faced each other at the door, and Diane knew she must follow.

He might take me to depths I have not yet known: there might truly be a hell with dark cells filled with scurrying vermin and forgotten humanity despairing of notice. Perhaps I'll rot in my cell. Perhaps I have no choice. Too late to ponder the consequences—my guide awaits.

"You know," said the pleasant-faced attendant helping her into the ambulance, "suicide is against the law." He walked off but soon appeared behind the wheel. The policeman jumped in beside her.

Are they taking me to jail? No, that can't be. Perhaps Bellevue, the modern Bedlam in Manhattan. That was it. But they said Metropolitan, and the ambulance was speeding uptown through the mocking brightness of the mid-morning sun.

"Why are you taking me to another hospital?" Diane asked the officer.

"They just want to talk to you, that's all."

"Will they let me leave?"

"Of course they will. Just talk to them, and let them know you're all right."

The panic began to rise; the implications of this solitary act grew in enormity. But as rapidly as the panic came, it receded, replaced by the knowledge of the futility of resistance and a strange sense of detachment, akin to curiosity. She leaned back in the ambulance and concentrated on the rocking motion of the vehicle, bouncing over the old, cobblestoned streets of Spanish Harlem.

Minutes later they were at the hospital, the attendant and policeman cautiously helping her down. They walked through corridors, bare and cold, and finally into the waiting area of the psychiatric unit, framed by the metal bars on the door.

They left her there, her keepers of the moment, and signed themselves out as she sat on a metal chair, waiting for the next keeper.

Presently, a rather large, friendly looking woman beckoned her into a small, barely furnished room. The woman adjusted her frame in the seat and stared at the papers on the desk before her. Her voice was gentle as she started her inquiry.

I don't want to talk, but I must. I have to convince her that I won't try this again, that I am capable of caring for myself. I must go home.

"Hello ... Diane Baker, is that right?

Diane nodded.

"My name is Mrs. Bailey. May I call you Diane?"

Diane nodded again.

"The doctors in the emergency room said you're depressed." Almost imperceptibly, she motioned at the papers before her. The evidence was formidable.

"Yes, I suppose I am."

"Why?"

Must I talk about it now? I can't put my life into one sentence. I can't say that my act was directed only against myself, that it didn't involve her, didn't involve anyone, for that matter. It was my solution—our freedom— David's and mine. But I must give her reasons and I must be coherent. I've got to make her sympathize with me, and yet I can't force her emotions. She's probably seen too many misfits to have much emotion left.

"This year … my divorce … David's absence. I guess I couldn't take it very well."

"Have you ever attempted suicide before?"

"No."

"Would you do it again?"

"No. I couldn't. What's going to happen to me now?"

"You're going to see the psychiatrist and then we'll decide what to do next. Please give me the name of a relative or friend to contact."

"I can't do that."

"Why not?"

"I couldn't impose myself on anyone."

"But surely there must be someone who would help you?"

Nancy would come as soon as she heard I needed her, but that's unfair to ask of her. Besides, how does one nurse a sick ego, an embarrassed admission of failure? No, that's out. Who else can I think of? She cast about in her mind for someone else while Mrs. Bailey waited. *Joan has her family to care about, and she's got so many problems of her own. And poor Michael would probably think himself responsible for this. David's gone, thank goodness. There's no one.*

"I don't want anyone to know about this. I'll manage myself."

"I must have someone's name. A family member?"

Diane said nothing. So far, so good. The joust seemed evenly matched.

"I'm afraid I'll have to recommend that you be sent to a hospital. You're hardly in a fit condition to care for yourself." The scales were suddenly shifting precariously.

Stay calm. She's testing me. She knows I'm rational but she wants to harass me, provoke me into a show of temper, and prove that I'm capable of further destruction. It's possible she considers suicide immoral … she may be determined to punish me for my unnatural act.

"Please, I can't stay in a hospital. It would only make things worse. I know it might be difficult at home, but I think I can manage." Diane's voice lowered at the last words, and her eyes turned down to look at her bandaged hands.

"I don't think we would be helping you if we sent you home." The kind voice had changed—it menaced her freedom with every word.

Diane leaned her head against the wall; the debate was over for the present. Her only chance seemed to be to convince the psychiatrist of her contrition, of her newly found will to live, albeit a feigned will. How much simpler things would have been if the attempt had been successful. No thoughts of hands and home or cheap excuses.

She lifted her head and looked at her inquisitor, wondering for the first time what this woman's function could be.

"May I ask … what you do? What's your title?" The query was timorously made.

"I'm a psychiatric social worker," Mrs. Bailey assured her.

Oh Lord, this can't be happening to me. I don't need a psychiatric social worker. I need David, but David is touring with the orchestra. Which one this time? The Vienna Philharmonic? Doesn't matter. He's playing to grateful audiences and spending his nights with Elizabeth. Tears began to form, but Diane fought them.

I must not break now. I must not weaken. She swallowed hard, her throat muscles tight, her mouth sour and dry. She forced David's image to recede, thinking again of the apartment and the bed where she could lay her tired head and sleep until this terrible fatigue left her body.

After a quick rap at the door, a man thrust his head into the room and signaled Mrs. Bailey, who rose quickly. "Coming, Doctor," she said and excused herself. This ended thoughts of a respite as the social worker joined the doctor in another room. Diane figured the social worker must be giving her evaluation to the doctor now. She thought the recommendation would be negative; it seemed the social worker was hostile to her. More questions would have to come, but maybe this would be the last interview. She knew she had to stay strong if she were to have a chance.

The social worker came back into the room. Mrs. Bailey asked Diane to follow her and led her to another small room, minimally furnished with a small desk, behind which the doctor sat, and two chairs. The room had that same dull grey quality that seemed to define the place. The doctor rose and introduced himself. "I'm Dr. Siegel. Please have a seat," he said as he extended his hand toward one of the chairs. He was young, almost her age, she thought. He had very blond hair and was so fresh looking, almost scrubbed to a polished finish, with big blue eyes peering out of a pale, plumpish face. Then he started to look angelic. She forced herself away from these thoughts. *It's the fatigue*, she thought. *I've got to stay awake and clear.* And, as though to agree with her thoughts, he started talking in a crisp though not altogether unsympathetic voice. "I'd like to ask you some questions and see if I can help you," he said in a calm, deliberate manner.

Should I be grateful? Should I smile pleasantly and introduce myself? He knows who I am; he's read the hospital report.

"It says here that you lacerated both wrists in an attempt on your life. Have you ever done anything like this before?"

"No, never."

"Have you been seeing a psychiatrist, Diane?"

"No."

"How long have you been feeling depressed?"

"Several months, I suppose. My divorce upset me. Everything changed so radically. I missed my husband though I … I had wanted the divorce. Even during our separation I missed him. We came together again, for a short time, but this time he wanted his freedom. I guess it really is over and I can't face it."

"May I ask why you wanted a divorce?"

"I thought … I thought I didn't love David anymore. I thought it was over. I … we … had met a man about two years ago. I became interested in him. I looked forward to seeing him, talking to him, with David, of course. Then I started becoming apprehensive when we met. I didn't know why. I found myself more conscious of my appearance. I began to look at myself more critically."

Diane looked down at her bandages, realized what she was doing, and forced herself to look the psychiatrist in the eye. "After a while I started to have fantasies about this man—sexual fantasies. We'd meet—alone—in my dreams, of course, and then it was always the perfection one dreams about. And all the time our lives, David's and mine, remained the same. Nothing changed except my thoughts, the fantasies that persisted in spite of myself."

I'm rambling. Maybe I've said too much. But he's waiting. He seems to expect more. "I love David. I loved him then but I didn't know it. I could only think that this must be the end of our love if I thought of another man, if I desired someone other than my husband. I felt guilty, disloyal … adulterous. That's an anachronism, isn't it?" She smiled ruefully, the melodrama of the word lightening the intensity of her feelings. "I suppose over everything was the feeling of confusion," she continued. "I couldn't talk about it to anyone. I felt alone."

"How long were you married, Diane?"

"We were married ten years."

"You were quite young when you married, weren't you?"

"Yes, only nineteen. David was twenty-five."

"What does David do?" asked Dr. Siegel, slightly leaning forward, as though he wanted to know more, wanted to involve himself more fully.

"He's a concert pianist."

"What are you doing now?"

"I've got a job with an ad agency. A few months ago I got a promotion, so I'm writing copy now."

"Do you like it?"

"I suppose so. I only had two years of college. I majored in English. Didn't know what else to do. The only thing I knew then was that I wanted to get out of the house, away from my family. David and I had been dating for a while—we'd gone to bed together. He was the first man, the only man I loved physically. It was a good marriage. We did love each other, but I … " She felt the words begin to tighten in her throat again. *The tears will come if I say much more about him.* Diane raised her eyes to look at the doctor's face. "This was a foolish thing to do. I see that now." *Please see how contrite I am.*

"Where is David now, Diane?"

"He's in South America."

"I see."

"You know, while you and the social worker were talking, I thought of a friend who could stay with me. I wouldn't have to be alone."

"What will you tell your friend?"

"I'll say I fell. That's not unreasonable."

"You want to go home very much, don't you?"

"Very much. I'd get depressed in a hospital. I'd hate myself for what I did—for losing my independence. I'm just starting to make a life. I've gotten a new apartment, one I really like. David and I had such different tastes; I always gave in to him on most matters. I'm only now starting to make decisions, and I suppose that frightens me. I think I've seen the worst, though. I think I can face it now."

"Would you consider psychiatric help, Diane?"

"Yes."

"All right. I'm going to recommend that you be allowed to go home. However, I want you followed on a regular basis. I expect you to start treatment, either here or with a psychiatrist of your own choosing. How does that sound to you?"

I need to say something before he changes his mind. "Thank you, Doctor. As soon as the bandages are off, I'll arrange to see someone."

He took out a paper from the pile in front of him and turned it toward her. "This is a release form I'd like you to sign. It absolves the hospital of any responsibility should there be any consequences due to your decision to leave. It's merely a formality," he said. "Can you manage it?"

"Sure," she said, as she slowly took the pen he extended to her.

"How are you planning on getting home?" he asked as he watched her slowly sign the form.

"I'll take a cab."

"Okay. When we exit the room, turn left and go down the corridor, then turn left again. You'll come to the front of the building. Cabs are coming and going regularly. You can get one there. And, good luck to you," he said as he rose and lifted the papers in front of him.

Diane rose also and started out. He walked quickly so as to arrive first at the door and open it for her. They left the room, and with a wave of his hand he was off, walking in the opposite direction.

Diane walked slowly and purposely down the corridor, savoring the sense of freedom that came with that wave that signaled his departure, his disappearance.

She got a taxi; the driver eagerly assisted her into the cab.

"How you doing?" said the driver.

Affecting a careless and self-mocking tone, she said, "Oh, I'm fine. I just had a stupid accident in my apartment and they fixed me up. I'll be better in no time." She was anxious to see if the lie possessed credibility.

The story of her clumsiness so impressed him he started regaling her with stories of his own clumsiness, as if he were trying to outdo her. Mercifully, the ride drew to an end and her doorman came forward to open the door.

However, he too, required an explanation. His sincere interest almost shamed her as she mumbled an abbreviated version of her fabrication and fled into the lobby, gratefully noticing it was empty. The two elevators were lit on the lobby floor, ready to be entered.

Upstairs she fitted her key into the lock and slowly turned it. Almost immediately she felt a stinging admonition in her wrist. She released her hand and looked about the empty corridor. Satisfied that no one was there to help her, she gripped the key in both hands, twisting her body in the direction of the key and pulling it round. Gratefully, she heard the familiar click.

The usually tidy apartment was in complete disarray, the chaos a silent affront to her oppressive need for order. This derangement of the familiar clouded her mental vision, increasing her hazy disbelief in her own act. She felt unbalanced, as though she were inhabiting an unknown land and encountering strange obstacles. She walked around the rooms, pushing bloodied clothes into a pile and awkwardly trying to hang those clothes thrown in haste on chairs and the unmade bed. Dirty dishes sat abandoned in the sink, half floating in cold, grey water, food and congealed grease crusted on rims. She tried to lift them and remove some globs of food, but that was too difficult. Nevertheless, the tasks were helping her compose her thoughts, bringing her nearer to a sense of her own world—to familiarity and routine.

But her arms were tired and the sling made everything more difficult. Besides, it was only one in the afternoon, and she'd been through what seemed like many days of tension. She sat on the couch wondering how she would care for herself for the next week if the most minute chore became an endurance test. She'd have to bathe and eat and try to keep the apartment in some semblance of order. Luckily, she'd watered the plants. But those were the only things that needed her care—a few pieces of vegetation.

She'd have to figure out ways to care for herself. She really didn't want to ask for help. She had made the psychiatrist think she would ask for help, but that wasn't going to happen. She'd maneuver this challenge alone.

The ringing phone ended her thoughts as she tried to lift the receiver from its cradle. The difficulty of extending her arms forced her to kneel on the floor.

"Hello."

"Hi, did I wake you? You sound sleepy."

"No, you didn't. I—

"Diane, is everything all right?"

"I had a little accident, Joan. Last night I was packing away some old things I don't use anymore and I had a rather freakish mishap."

"Are you all right now?"

"Yes, I'm fine. There's nothing to worry about."

"Was anything broken?"

"No. I just cut some skin, that's all.

"Do you want me to come and help you with anything?"

"No, really. Everything's under control."

"Are you sure you don't want me to come up?"

"Yes, really."

"Look, why don't you come down? The kids are with Mitchell and we could talk."

She didn't want to leave the comfort of the apartment, nor have Joan see the apartment in this condition. But Joan interrupted her thoughts with what seemed like a stifled sob. "I need to talk to someone. Please come down?" It was a plea she couldn't ignore. If she didn't let her come up, or if she didn't go down, it would look suspicious. She looked longingly at the apartment and thought of the bed and how she would welcome a few hours of sleep. She needed the rest, but she couldn't leave things this way. Too blunt, too cold.

"All right, give me a few minutes."

The lie was getting easier. The rest shouldn't be too difficult. Maybe walking herself to the hospital on Lenox Avenue, weary with bruised and inflamed wrists early this morning, was the most difficult part, even though the hospital was only a few blocks from where she lived. Maybe even just walking into the emergency room was the most difficult part. *It just has to get better*, she thought with a deep sense of despair and resignation. *Or does it just keep getting worse?* But the job now was to go down to Joan's, quickly, before she came up.

She lifted herself from the floor and walked into the bathroom. The tub, still streaked with dried blood, was an affront to her aborted attempt at escape. Looking into the mirror, she noticed how wan she was, how disheveled her hair looked. She splashed some water on her face and then took the comb and slowly pulled it through her hair, dropping her head to let the comb reach her hair. She put some Vaseline on her lips and patted them to remove some of the oil. Only partially satisfied with the results, she left the apartment.

Double locking her door seemed too great a feat for the moment, so she just closed it and took the elevator two flights down. Even ringing Joan's bell was a difficult task; she kicked the door with her foot, frustration and anger contributing to the force.

Joan's presence at the door forcibly dispelled her indignation. She would play the clumsy fool, castigating herself for her carelessness—or was it her bad fortune?

Joan sympathetically escorted her to the couch, insisting that she place a stuffed pillow under the sling-encased arm and another one under the free one.

"It really looks a lot worse than it is," Diane explained.

"How exactly did it happen?"

"You know, I can't really remember. It happened so fast."

"It must have been terribly painful. When did you go to the doctor's?"

"Well, when it happened it didn't seem very bad, so I went to sleep. Besides, it was late last night. This morning my wrists hurt, so I went to the emergency room. In a few days the bandages will come off. Really, it not very bad, so let's stop talking about it."

"Nothing's broken then?"

"No. Now tell me what's been happening to you."

"Well, you know Mitch's been dating someone regularly now and he has the kids today. Well … get this. He wanted to take the kids for the weekend, and his girlfriend—" she said this with an impatient gesture of her hand, almost like the word was a nasty one—"was going to stay over with them. Naturally, I said no. How can he be so insensitive? The kids aren't even used to this arrangement, and he wants to introduce them to his new playmate. I was furious." She looked furious. Her face was almost twisted, her mouth hard and drawn.

"I can't understand it," Joan continued. "I wonder why he's so oblivious to their needs. I'm starting to think Mitchell is incapable of thinking of anyone but himself at the moment. That's not true. I think he always thought of himself only, and I went along. But I refused to agree to this request—after all, I have to think of the children." She was working herself into a frenzy; her voice was rising and it was starting to look like this might never end.

Diane wished she was alone in the apartment. Her wrists were beginning to hurt, her head was aching, and she was so tired. She just didn't want to hear any more of this rant. And, as if an answer to a prayer, Joan's voice abruptly changed from one of anger to that of friendly concern.

"Diane, have you eaten?"

"I'm really not very hungry."

"Look, Mitchell's going to be eating with the kids. I'm starting to get hungry. Why don't you have something with me."

Diane hesitated.

"You'd be doing me a favor. I hate eating alone, and I probably wouldn't have anything if you weren't here."

"I don't want you to bother. I don't really have much of an appetite."

"No bother. We'll just have a light bite."

Joan walked into the kitchen and Diane remained on the couch, glad for the sudden silence. Her eye caught sight of a few toys that had escaped Joan's cleaning efforts. They looked mischievous, peeking out from under chairs. The foyer walls were full of the children's bright-colored finger paintings; they made the apartment look merry. Children could do that—add cheer, create a sense of future. *Joan is lucky—she isn't alone*, thought Diane.

Why didn't we have children? We don't have the time for a baby, David had said. But I had the time. The baby would take something away from us, from our love, he had insisted. We don't need anything more, he'd said, but I did. I wanted a baby, something of the both of us, something more to love.

Joan called from the kitchen, announcing dinner.

Diane started eating, but the cold chicken tasted dry, and swallowing became an almost painful effort.

"Joan, would you forgive me? I'm tired and I'm not at all hungry? I think I'd just like to go upstairs and lie down."

"Are you all right?"

"Yes, just a bit tired."

More assurances were necessary before Joan would let her leave.

"I'll call you in the morning. But you will call me if you need anything, won't you?"

"I promise."

Chapter 2

JOAN CLEARED THE TABLE, LOADING THE DISHWASHER with the soiled utensils. The sounds of the appliance broke the silence in the apartment, but then the steady drone of the machine blended with the sounds that entered the darkened rooms. She could hear the strident blast of the whistle as the doorman hailed a taxi, or a fire engine or police car raced through the streets, heralded by the formidable siren's wail. Small moments of quiet were broken by drivers furiously blowing their car horns.

The sounds, constant companions of city life, reached the darkened apartment on the tenth floor with muffled harshness, the space diffusing and spreading the dissonant reports of the activity below. The smothered clamor filled the rooms and made them emptier, the absence of voices giving greater clarity to the inanimate sounds.

Joan poured herself a glass of red wine and brought it to the couch. She huddled into the thick fabric of the overstuffed sofa and took a large gulp. It warmed her and she continued drinking, dreamily looking out at the lights of the apartments across the wide street. Soon, the brilliance began to blur, blending gently with the half glow of the city-lit night. She began to let go of her will. Her languid body eased further into the couch as the recollection of a happier time tantalized her sad spirit. And as if a dream would suffice, the scene changed. Her mind's eye was filling the apartment with the children's presence, their arrival preceded by their laughter, loud and infectious. She rushed to embrace her babies, her specters no longer babies but sweet children, still ready to be lavished with adoration and affection.

The lovely dream went on. Now they were getting the children to bed, laughing with the loving effort, hugging and kissing and sometimes tenderly tickling the children in their soft pajamas in their delicately lit rooms. Squeals of delight from their children, too happy to sleep, and then more embraces laced with love and whispers, and finally, soft blankets brought to tiny chins, gifted with more kisses.

The day had ended well, and if they weren't too tired, she and Mitchell would make love. They were rarely too tired for that, except for the last few weeks. The sweet reverie continued warm and comfortable, like the imagined tub she was in, with bath water sprinkled with sweet oil, its lingering redolence bringing to mind the image of a tropical flower, pendulous with vibrant-hued petals. She soaked her body until her skin was soft, the palms of her hands wrinkled like velvet pink prunes. The warm water swished gently around her body, massaging like a thousand tiny fingers. The water touched her breasts, not quite reaching her nipples but now and again rippling close, then drawn away with a lingering sense of a gentle caress.

At last, languorous and sleepy, she left the tub, wrapping her body in the large, lush terry towel. She stood still, warm and comfortable, not willing to release herself from the towel embracing her body. Finally, she started rubbing her skin, and the last moisture of the fragrant bath was transferred to the towel. She pulled on the nightgown, half smiling at the way it would surely be discarded. She drew a matching robe over the filmy gown and opened the bathroom door. A draft of cool air blew into the warmed and misty room and chilled her for a moment. She waited while the mirror's mist cleared, and then she combed her hair, finishing with a dab of perfume behind her ears.

She went into the bedroom, lifted the covers, and slipped in beside Mitchell. He was engrossed in a law journal, almost unaware of his wife's presence. She touched his shoulder, and he turned toward her, putting the journal on the side table. His hands reached out and she was drawn into his arms, his lips touching hers, and then moving to her neck and her breasts. Her hands moved down his body, feeling the hardness of his hip, the strong, muscular leg, and his sex growing hard and large.

Their bodies joined, and they started the slow, sinuous movements that rapidly increased with each thrust, the exquisite paroxysms coming at the height of the desperate ecstasy. Now Mitchell was moaning in a frenzy of motion, at last expelling his substance and his breath in a final thrust.

Softened from the rigidity of a moment ago, he lay tired and limp above her. She moved beneath him, and he remembered her. He rolled over on his side, drawing her to him, holding her close, their arms encircling each other.

The sound of a key in the lock forced Joan out of her reverie. With an effort she lifted herself from the couch and turned the lamp on, blinking her eyes in the sudden light. The children tramped into the apartment, pulling off clothes and dropping them on the nearest chair. She looked at her watch in disbelief, noticing the lateness of the hour. The children would be exhausted in the morning, their schedule completely ruined. Anger welled up in her, and cool reason was discarded by the irrational belief that Mitchell was determined to decimate their lives, abetted by a shadowy figure of a woman who conspired with him to negate his wife's every wish. She was too angry to respond with her usual outstretched arms as Jason and Melinda started toward her.

"Go into your rooms this instant and get into your pajamas. It's too late for a bath."

The children rushed away from her, alarmed by her harsh tone, bewildered by this unexpected attitude. They fled to their rooms.

Joan directed her flashing eyes toward Mitch. "How dare you keep them out so late! You know they have school in the morning. How can they be expected to be normal children if they aren't treated that way?"

How abruptly the dream had been torn from her, the unseen fissure gashed and jagged. They hadn't spent the day together; they hadn't enjoyed the contented leisure of a Sunday afternoon. She had remained behind, alone and separate, apart from them.

Mitch was silent, surprised by the onslaught and unwilling to argue. He stood there, just looking at her. This silence, at once stoic and stubborn, held a trace of mockery. It fueled her resentment.

"I don't know if I even want them to see you anymore. I don't think this arrangement is good, not at all. They see you for a day and then you're gone, a visitor they call 'Daddy'. Why don't you get out of here and leave us alone? Just get out of our lives!" Her voice had risen. .

"I'm sorry, Joan. I hadn't realized it was quite this late. I went to a restaurant, and somehow between bad service and a little fun, it was later than I had intended."

His beseeching voice washed over her rage, subduing the anger ready to erupt again at real or imagined provocation. He even offered to help her put the children to sleep. Surely this was reminiscent of a happier day—or perhaps a dream?

The children were tired and cranky, and helping them with nightly rituals and into bed took longer than usual, their disagreeable homecoming the reason for resisting their mother's efforts to touch them. Finally, they were in bed and asleep, the day's joy turned to sadness and confusion and, in the morning, the inevitable loss of their father.

Joan moved close to the edge of the bed, as far away as possible from Mitchell's sleeping form. She turned her head into the pillow, trying to smother the sobs that shook her body. *I'll wake him and he'll see me crying, and he mustn't see that,* she thought in a panic. It was wrong to have had sex with him, she knew. Her vulnerability had left her defenseless. And he with a girlfriend, too. So, for this night, he had both, she thought, with a terrible hatred of herself. He had used her and she hated him for it. She got out of the bed, her tall, lissome figure nearly bowed with an invisible burden. Her dejection sapped her strength.

She walked into the darkened living room, the familiar objects partly discernible in the diffused light emanating from the street. She sat on the sofa, leaning against the stuffed pillows as if they could shelter her somehow from the pain that was starting to grow anew.

"We could live together, the way it always was," he said after making love and holding her tenderly. His hands caressed her hair and her cheek. His lips kissed her brow, moistened from the lovemaking. *When did it happen?* she wondered. *First, we were putting the children in pajamas and putting them to sleep, and then we were in bed making love as though it were any other night.* "Nothing has to change. I've thought it over, and I can't see anything objectionable about what we'll do," his cajoling voice continued. "There's no need to split up. It's hurting us and the children. If we stayed together, we could enjoy the life we've always had and still do our own thing."

She started to stiffen, his last words implying another necessary accommodation to change, another modification in her life to please Mitchell. Why had she ever let him in her bed again? Was she so low that a few sweet words could change her heart, when she really knew it was no longer a marriage, when she knew he was repugnant to her, when she knew she must change her life and start anew? She was so tired, so sapped of her normal nature. It was all so quick. One moment she was happy, fulfilled, doing what she always did—being a mother and wife and occasionally a substitute teacher—and the next moment it was lawyers and dollars and arrangements and anything that was disruptive. It was so hard and she was so tired.

She thought back to just a few minutes ago in the bed, held by her former husband—lover, partner. Mitch had gone on speaking, caressing her. Her passive silence hadn't stopped him. His lips that brushed across her brow, his firm hold, his hands that caressed her, it all began to feel like sandpaper, rubbing harshly along her body, his lips like gnats gnawing away at her flesh. The constant repetition of the strokes of endearment, ordinarily welcome, were now abrasive. She had started to move, but Mitchell grasped her more firmly and started talking faster, his voice rising.

"This is good, Joan, and you liked it too. We could have it this way whenever we wanted, but we'd still be free to go our own way, have our own friends—all right, sex partners. People need diversity, Joan. Marriage isn't a natural state. Not for you either. We don't need to resent our freedom. We don't have to break our family up because of our personal needs."

Joan remained silent. She was afraid that if she tried to talk, all that would come out would be a wrenching scream. She pulled herself away, turning her back to him. She could tell he propped himself up, wondering what to do next. *Don't touch me*, her mind screamed. *I couldn't bear that now.*

"Joan, let's talk about it … please. I don't want to hurt you or the children. This is hurting me too. Joan, I don't want our marriage to end."

"Please stop, Mitchell. I don't even want to think about what you're saying.

Go to sleep. Just try and leave before the children wake up. I don't want them to assume anything hopeful from your presence. They've got to get used to their new status."

"Joan, I—"

"Please, Mitchell, let's not talk anymore."

With an almost inaudible sign of resignation, he turned on his side. Soon she heard his heavy, regular breathing, which only disturbed her further. Perhaps she had become accustomed to sleeping alone, or maybe the day's events had simply been too overwhelming. There was the rush to get the children ready in the morning, and then Mother's call. *I suppose Mother thinks I should put on black and wait for the end of my days. She almost implied that. Well, she had a good marriage, so she expected I would. And she had a good relationship with Mitchell. She saw his lighter side, the sweet side, because he really seemed to care for her.*

Then her mind went to Diane's accident. She seemed so helpless and was alone too. Diane's aloneness seemed to call for confirmation of her children's existence, so she walked into their rooms, looking at the sleeping faces and silently chastising herself for berating them for their father's faults.

She drew the covers closer to Jason's face, noticing the healing scar on his cheek and smiling to herself as she remembered how he clung to her after he fell coming off the slide a few days ago. She kissed his sleep-warmed face and adjusted the blanket, the one he still loved even though he was six now.

She walked to Melinda's room, pink and full of the dolls she played with. She was sleeping deeply, her dark curls framing her face and giving her the cherubic look Joan loved. Guilty with the hurt she had inflicted, she left her little girl's room with the determination to spare her children her agony. She'd never scream at them again, not the way she did when they came home. Poor children. It wasn't their fault, and yet they had to suffer her hurt. Not ever again, she vowed, would she put them through that, hoping even then that she could keep that promise.

They'd build a future, but it would be without Mitchell. She'd start a new life for herself, even plan a new career, but she'd think about that tomorrow. For now, she needed sleep. Perhaps a pill to ensure her rest or make the sleep heavier. Maybe some wine would help even more than the pill.

Chapter 3

Diane woke to the shrill sound of the ringing phone on her night table. Stretching her arm to reach it, she was rudely reminded of her limitations. She rolled over on her side and then lifted herself from the bed, the phone ringing with what sounded like a desperate urgency. She picked up the receiver wondering who would be calling this early.

"Hello."

Diane, are you all right?"

"Stuart ... I'm sorry. I was so tired I dozed off last night and just forgot to set the alarm. I meant to call the office at 9:00." She looked at the clock on the table. It was 10:30. Her friends at the office must have wondered what happened to her. She should have called Hal, a supervisor whom she liked and with whom she worked well.

"I had a slight accident."

"Are you all right?"

"Yes, just somewhat incapacitated. My hands are bandaged. I don't think I'll be coming to work for several days."

"Slight accident? It doesn't sound so slight. What did you do?"

"Oh ... just my own stupidity. I was putting some stuff away ... just ... stupid. I don't even want to talk about it. Just one of those dumb things."

"Okay ... do you need anything?"

"No, I'm fine really, and I have a friend living in the building who's been really helpful." *This little lie can't hurt. Besides, Joan is really trying to help.*

"Do you think you'd like some company tonight? I've had this urge for Chinese food. We could picnic in your charming apartment."

"I don't know about tonight. Maybe another night."

"Diane, we both have to eat. You won't be making dinner, and I want to see you to be sure you're okay."

"All right, Stuart. Come on up about seven.

"It's a date."

"Oh, Stuart, please let me talk to Hal."

She repeated her story to Hal, who listened sympathetically.

"Take all the time you need," he told her, straining to keep his voice congenial. She knew the Philo account was due in a few days and they were behind schedule on the Benson layout. *It was rotten luck ... she was rotten luck*, she thought ruefully.

"I'll call you in a few days, Hal. Maybe the bandages will be off and I'll be able to come in."

"You take care now and don't worry about anything. *Ciao*, baby."

"Bye, Hal, and thanks."

Poor Hal. He'll be in for it this week, she thought regretfully as she hung up the phone with both hands. Diane began to ready herself for a bath, wondering how she'd maneuver so as not to wet the bandages. She was taking fresh underclothes out of the drawer when the phone rang again. This time it was Nancy, another caring friend.

"I called you at the office, but they said you weren't in yet. Is everything all right?"

"I had a freakish accident. I fell on my wrists, some skin was broken. They sewed it up and then bandaged the hands so the stitches wouldn't come loose. It really sounds and looks much worse than it is."

"Do you need anything? Can you manage?"

"I'm doing fine. A friend from the office is coming over tonight with dinner. Joan, she lives downstairs, she offered to get me anything

I need, so I'm sort of taken care of. The bandages should be off in a few days."

"You're sure there's nothing I can do for you."

"No, really. How's Larry?" Diane asked, genuinely interested in Nancy's husband, a man she liked and respected, as did David.

"He's fine. We went to Connecticut on Sunday. Saw Roberta and the kids, and Larry played golf with Joel. I've got to go now. My other phone's ringing. Call me if you need anything."

"I will. Good-bye."

Why did I agree to Stuart's visit tonight? I'll have to sit here and recount the whole story, blood and all. He's kind, though, and he has been a good friend.

When she had first come to the agency, shy and uncertain, Stuart had taken her under his wing. Before long they were lunching together, talking about each other's lives, especially Stuart's polygamous existence with his many male lovers. He was easy to talk to and usually sympathetic. Sometimes his exaggerated motions and media jargon would irk her, but she shrugged it off as pettiness on her part. Tonight, however, he'd probably grate on her nerves; she wasn't in the mood for pretense, his or hers.

She started toward the bath again when the phone rang for the third time. Now it was Joan inquiring about her night and her current needs.

"I'm fine and so far the fridge is full. How did things go last night with you and Mitchell?"

"Not very well … "

"What happened?"

"It was awful … I was awful … I can't even … "

I don't want to hear this. Please don't let this go on. But what can I do?

"Look, how about coming up and having lunch with me? We can talk about it then," said Diane, almost crisply. She wanted to be off the phone, to end the conversation, and now she'd just invited her to continue it. It didn't seem like a choice, just a necessity.

"All right."

"Make it in about an hour. I just got up."

She wants to talk. I don't really want to listen, but she sounded sad and tired. Something must have happened.

She took a partial shower; it was a cumbersome affair. Even drying herself was difficult. Her morning ritual took longer than she had anticipated. Every action was reduced to slow motion.

She found some old jeans, stretched with age, and drew them on. Last night's blouse would have to suffice. In fact, for the duration of the disability, these same clothes would do. The blouse could be washed and dried rapidly, and the loose-fitting jeans were easy to get on and off.

She had just enough time to start pouring juice when the doorbell rang.

"Hi," Joan said without enthusiasm. She stared hard at Diane. "Boy, you look as drained as I feel," she said, wondering to herself now about the bandaged hands.

Diane forced herself to smile.

"I brought some muffins. I'll make us coffee, " Joan said, realizing the former remark wasn't one she should have made.

"There's jam and cheese in the fridge if you want."

Joan busied herself in the tiny kitchen, doing with ease what Diane realized would have taken her far more time to manage.

"Joan, what happened last night? You seem upset."

"I am upset. That bastard wants us to live together, everything exactly as before, only now we're free to come and go as we please … you know, choose our own sex partners, experiment with other people, multiple partners, kinky sex … whatever we want … " Her voice trailed off, caught in a sob. "That lousy bastard! I'll show him. He'll pick those kids up in the lobby. He's not going to set foot in my apartment again, and anything he wants to tell me will be through a lawyer."

"But, Joan, the kids are going to be hurt."

"The kids are going to learn what kind of a son of a bitch their father is, and if now is the time, so be it."

Obviously, there would be no reasoning with Joan this morning.

She'll come round and realize she can't use the children for her vengeance. No sense telling her that now though. She wouldn't even listen.

Joan switched subjects, sensing Diane's emotional distance. "I wish they would have called me today to teach. I would have welcomed that. I could have used the diversion … and the money. I'd like to see my analyst more often."

"Maybe I should see an analyst too. I just don't know what it would do for me … what I would achieve. What has it done for you?"

Joan smiled, relaxed after venting about her husband.

"I don't really know. I look forward to seeing him. I can tell him things I can't really tell anyone else, and I suppose that relieves me. Sometimes it makes me see things in a different perspective … you know, like viewing the situation from afar. I suppose I'm looking to him for the answers to my screwed-up life. He can't bring the past back, I know that. Maybe I can learn to live in the future—a bit more successfully."

Joan was moving around the little kitchen, taking plates, cups, and silver from the cupboards and drawers and putting them on the table in the dining area. She moved briskly, almost as though her anger, now freshly refueled by new thoughts of Mitchell, was giving her strength and energy. "You know, sometimes I'm even glad Mitchell and I broke up. I can't even explain it to myself. I'm doing things I never did before. C'mon, let's sit down. I think we have everything we need," she said, surveying the table and the contents. "Wait, do you want milk? I didn't take that out of the fridge."

"Yes, please," said Diane, watching Joan remove a carton of milk. It was all so easy for Joan, she thought, but that easy task would mean opening the door with two hands and carrying that quart carton, which looked like a gallon of lead to Diane, with both hands.

Joan sat down at the table. "What I was saying, about doing things I never did before … this may sound foolish, but it meant a lot to me. Mitchell never liked my hair short, and I always wanted to get a real close-cropped cut. Well, after we split up, I went into the salon and had them cut away, and when it was over I felt a bit bald, but victorious too. I love it. It feels so free and needs so little care. But it was really more than just a different hairstyle; it was knowing that I wasn't pleasing anyone but myself. Do you know what I mean?" She looked at Diane.

"Yes, I do."

"Do you know what else I've been thinking about? I never really liked teaching. The money is good, the hours are convenient, but I'm bored by it. I've been thinking of making some sort of change. The only problem is that I don't know what I'd like to do."

Diane nodded. "I remember when my brother, Steve, was undecided about what career to pursue. My parents took him for aptitude tests. I think it was during his sophomore year in college. Anyway, they did confirm the fact that medicine was a distinct possibility. The counselor made a few other suggestions, but of course, my parents were pleased to know Steve had an aptitude for medicine. He loves it, and they're so proud of him. Actually, though, he's so proud of himself, they hardly get to talk to him. I've ended up as their emissary when they have messages or need anything from him." Diane smiled wryly.

She moved her hand and Joan pushed the apricot jam toward her. "Oh, no thanks, I was headed for the butter," Diane said, smiling broadly at her clumsiness. "I can't wait for these things to come off."

"When is that?"

"About three more days. It's not that bad. I'm getting used to it. Don't worry about it. I was talking about Steve, but what I wanted to say was that aren't daughters gifts for parents in their old age? We're supposed to be tender and minister to their needs. Well, not right now," she said with another smile. "But they always considered my home as an extension of theirs, but Steve's was a sacred temple they entered only when the god commanded. And it wasn't as though Allie wasn't friendly. She simply took her cue from Steve. After all, he wasn't very interested in them, so why should she be interested?"

"More coffee?" Joan asked.

Diane nodded and went on talking. "Sometimes after a visit there, a rare visit, they'd call me and complain about how they were treated. They never minced words of criticism for me, but they'd cut their tongues out before they would openly say a word against Allie or Steve. They're afraid of him. They think he's so rich and busy that they're actually indebted to him when he phones or, on those rare occasions, when he deigns to see them. No wonder Allie's glad to be free. He must be a pompous ass to live with."

"Wow, it sounds like there's not a whole lot of love between you both."

Diane took another sip of coffee. "I really do love my brother. I remember when we were kids, and even in college. He was a super brother and I looked up to him. I still love him, but he's distant now and Mr. Big." Her voice trailed off. "You know, Joan," she said pensively, "I think I'm jealous of him. Even without the kids, Steve's got a purpose and an interest. He's invariably complaining about how busy he is and how he doesn't have a moment to call his own, but he loves his work. *Really loves it.* You could tell when the answering service would call, and we'd all be at dinner. He loved the sense of importance those calls gave him. He'd leave the table, theatrically perturbed and graciously apologetic. I think now and then he would mumble how they just don't leave him alone. Of course, I would argue that he and his colleagues have made medicine an exclusive club, but he's adamant. Says things like, 'Can't change the system overnight—have to watch our standards,' et cetera."

Unthinkingly, Diane was imitating Steve's deeper voice and inflection. She shrugged and resumed her normal speech pattern. "Allie never minded the fees he took from patients, but she resented the time he gave them. And what did she have to do? Nothing. Just get the latest designer label, frost her hair a different shade every week, and do some volunteer work for some well-known cause—"

"Wait a minute," Joan interrupted. "Don't they have kids?"

"Yes, but Steve always got the kids up at the crack of dawn and got them ready. They were gone by the time Allie wandered downstairs."

"Did they have a nanny for the kids?"

"Steve doesn't like that, but Allie managed to have care for them in the afternoons, and then there was always the housekeeper to fall back on."

Diane was twisting her torso now, trying to retrieve the napkin that had slid off her lap.

"I'll get that," said Joan as she picked it up. "I'll get you another one."

"No, it's fine. Wasn't there more than five seconds," she said with a smile.

Joan adjusted herself in her chair again and lifted the cup with a sigh. "Allie didn't have it so bad. What bothered her?"

"I think it was just … enough of Steve and the whole thing. It was boring her and making her restless. You really wouldn't recognize her now," Diane said with a wry smile. "Wears nothing but jeans and Indian blouses and even let her natural color grow in. A dull brown, but it's all hers. Anyway, it a change."

"What about the children?" asked Joan.

"She wants Steve to take them. Full time, not just now and then. Actually, since she moved out there hasn't been too much of a problem. The cleaning lady became their housekeeper and the children's lives weren't as disrupted as they might have been. Allie wants to go back to school. Get a PhD in one of the sciences. She doesn't want to go back to nursing, and she doesn't want to teach."

"I can understand that," said Joan with conviction.

As they were finishing breakfast, Diane suggested they move to the couch. Joan got up to clear the table.

"Leave it. I can do it later," Diane said. "Really, I can. It might take a few more minutes but I'll do it. Come, let's sit on the couch. Take my coffee for me."

"Okay, but let me put some things in the fridge," which she did quickly.

Diane got up from the table and walked to the couch. Joan followed with their cups, which she placed on the coffee table. Then she sat down on a large plush chair, the soft filling and fabric molding to her body, making her look limp and sleepy. Diane was talking again, but she could see Joan was getting tired. She had put some of David's music on the CD player—what was it, a Bach concerto? It was making her drift also. She didn't want to get sleepy, so she started talking. "I never thought in terms of a career. I guess emotionally and financially I went from my father to David. Except for his practice sessions, David and I were always together. I was content just to be with him … " Her voice trailed off and she stopped talking and looked down. When she saw her hands, she closed her eyes for a minute and then quickly looked up to see the tenderness on Joan's face.

Don't look at me like that, Diane thought. *Don't forget your anger, Joan. Let me talk about David and Steve. Now let me have a show of anger. It's okay. Really, it's okay. I haven't talked about it for so long and I need to talk about it.*

But she didn't say that. She just looked at her friend silently, almost as though she sensed the care and didn't want to burden her further. *Poor Joan,* she thought. *I've got to stop this. Besides, it's useless to talk of these things now. What good will it do?*

Except for the music, the room was quiet. Joan waited for Diane to fill the awkward silence.

"I have to do some shopping," Joan suddenly announced, almost shaking herself from the lethargy that seemed to be overtaking her. "Can I get you anything?"

"I don't think so. I have just about everything I need. Thanks, though, I do appreciate your asking."

"Is there anything you want me to do for you now?"

"No, I'm just going to take it easy. Maybe I'll watch some television or read. Stuart's coming with dinner about seven. I'll just relax till then. Thanks for looking in and for lunch."

Joan left after cleaning the dishes and table, in spite of Diane's protestations about being able to do it all.

"I'll call later, just to make sure everything's okay," Joan promised.

"Thanks, Joan."

Diane was relieved when she heard the door close behind her. Joan's anger often was like an unquenchable fire, and sometimes she could feel those flames trying to reach out and sear her also. Joan restrained herself before she got too wound up this time, she thought. She'd be too difficult to handle now if she hadn't controlled herself, though Diane felt as though she filled the morning with her own ashes of despair. She and Joan were feeding each other, and the fuel could have become corrosive. It was good to be alone now.

She walked over to the computer, but she could do nothing with bad hands. She looked at the television guide and decided there was little of interest there—old movies, a few soap operas, and some game shows. She wished she had the magazine or entertainment section of the *Times*. She browsed through her book shelf, her eyes stopping on *Faust*. Painfully, she wrested the book from the shelf and brought it to the couch. It was a familiar story to her, one of her favorites. She also loved that opera. The final scene always brought her to some sense of satisfied completion. It was almost on a otherworldly level, this heightened sense of pleasure with the music, the chorus, and the ultimate sense of justice. It all rose in an almost spiritually orgasmic climax.

I wonder why I'm so fascinated by this story, then and now. Perhaps we both faced death and made conscious choices. Margaret didn't retreat. I retreated. I remember that moment when I thought I might succeed at ending it all.

Diane knew she needed to consider what she had done. It was painful, but she let her mind go over the bloody details. Besides, she couldn't stop the thoughts or even change the pictures forming in her mind's eye. Maybe it would make sense if she let it go on.

She saw the rush of blood, she felt the fright, like it was happening that moment. Her mind went back to the act, and she remembered her sense of sinking into an emptiness more fearful than the one she was in. She remembered how she felt she could change her mind then, stop it all, but then she noticed the blood clotting and she became angry knowing it all might be a failure. She slashed again, but to no avail. She had bypassed the vital vein. Now she looked down at her bandaged hands, thinking what a sad compensation they were for a return to life.

She sat on the couch, holding the book but not opening it. The music of the opera ran through her mind, but the pitiable words of Faust needed no accompaniment.

I wonder if I'd sell my soul in return for happiness, Diane thought.

No chance. The devil hasn't offered you any terms, an inner voice answered.

Would I want David's love, years of uninterrupted joy in exchange for ... what?

This isn't the Middle Ages. Be sensible, she chided herself. *I've got to start living without David and for myself.*

But that's a meaningless existence, she argued with the voice within. *I can't live without purpose and David was my purpose. Being loved and loving him was sufficient.*

Then why did I start questioning that love? Why did I become critical of David, apparently without justification?

But there was justification; he was selfish, he rarely cared about my needs, small as they were. He wanted unquestioning love, a constant confirmation of his worth. My adoration of him became too heavy a burden, for both us. I couldn't ignore the gnawing and oppressive sense of loss, the loss of myself in him. It always seemed it was his needs I cared about, his need for confirmation of his worth. I never felt he cared about me the way I cared about him.

Even as these thoughts flowed through her mind, other thoughts of joyous moments of his caring interrupted, like the tempting furies of another truth.

That time when I thought he had forgotten my twenty-fifth birthday. I remember as if it were yesterday. We had plans for dinner with his friend Richard, the ranting, one-book novelist. He was always going on about the mediocrity of the intellectual community and that there was a special place for genius in a capitalistic world. Richard was our trial, but David loved him.

She shifted on the couch, the book tumbling from her lap, but she didn't notice. She was remembering how she thought the dinner would be a sad affair, Richard's debts probably the main topic of conversation, or his writer's block. She was not looking forward to hearing about his involvement in several current and past relationships. He always drank heavily and seemed bent on destroying himself. It would be a trying evening, and Diane remembered feeling dejected and disappointed about David's lack of thought about her birthday.

When they reached Richard's apartment, Diane noticed there was no light showing through the door, and she heard no sounds from the other side. Possibly Richard had forgotten they were coming. Well, they could probably have a Chinese dinner in that small place on Columbus Avenue. That would be so much better. Diane was disappointed when Richard did open the door, but then she heard voices shouting, "Surprise!" Friends were rushing toward her, laughing and reaching for her. David stood by, smiling with an air of satisfaction she rarely saw. She caught his eye, and he returned her look with a grin from ear to ear, looking happy and boyish. They were brought into the living room with shouts and laughter, and the evening was filled with humor and wine and the hot Indian dishes that Diane and David loved. David had planned all that, probably taking time out from a practice session or two, to oversee her night.

I loved that night the most, Diane decided, *because David had worked so hard to make it a special evening for me. And later, at home, he gave me that beautiful scarf I had admired weeks before in a small shop on Third Avenue. It was a delicate handcraft with embroidered flowers in bright colors. I hadn't thought of it for myself, it was too expensive, the work so fine. I remember he smiled so mysteriously as I opened the beautiful box and laughed with satisfaction as I covered my face with it.*

We made love that night with a fervor I hadn't known for a long time, though our lovemaking was always beautiful. Only toward the end of our marriage did Mark's image mar my pleasure.

Chapter 4

DIANE'S HEAD DROPPED ONTO THE BACK OF the sofa, her eyes closed. The darkness lasted only a minute, though. She had transported herself to a tropical, primeval forest. She was running along a mossy path, dwarfed by the great trees on both sides. The air was thick with the scent of blossoms, and a light mist covered everything. Now and then the sun's rays would wend their way through the lush verdancy, illuminating everything in their path. She was alone and naked in the forest, and as she ran she threw out her arms and lifted her head, the wind whispering in her hair.

Soon she stopped and with a happy laugh threw herself to the ground. She noticed some ferns embracing a tree trunk, so she leaned her body against the tree, the ferns like textured velvet against her back. Birds hovered nearby and whistled or sang, filling the forest with music, spontaneous and joyful.

She spied some fruit hanging from a tree, the golden skin ready to burst with the ripe substance of the fruit. She picked the fruit and bit deep into the core, the juice running out and spilling down her chin. She wiped her chin with a leaf, but the golden juice ran with every bite. It was a tasty fruit, full of rich sweetness.

After her succulent treat she wandered away from the tree, eager to explore the lovely forest further. Thinking she heard the gurgling of water, she walked in the direction of the sound. Trees fanned her skin with cool breezes and now and then wiped the moisture from her flesh with outstretched leaves.

Flashes of light turned leaves gold and crimson. Dew drops sparkled like tiny prisms, reflecting light from their delicate, ephemeral bodies before they were blown away by the brush of the wind.

She roamed on, the bubbling of the water becoming louder. At last she was in a clearing of sorts. Large purple flowers ringed the forest, and a soft, grassy fringe skirted a flowing stream. She followed the stream, spying a waterfall, almost hidden by trees and foliage.

She advanced to the waterfall, kneeling near the edge of the rippling stream while the sun blazed on the water cascading down the rocks, illuminating the falls with radiant light. She cupped her hands and brought the clear, cool liquid to her mouth. A mist rising out of the falls cooled her warm body. Refreshed, she strolled away from the falls, wandering deeper into another forest. Now, crimson-colored cardinals, bright cockatoos, and bluebirds flew close to her, seeming to guide her way.

Feeling drowsy again, she looked for a spot to rest. She entered a glade, the grass looking soft and inviting. She slipped down, the earth's mattress as delicate as goose feathers. Her lids became heavy and she closed them, surrendering herself to the earth, which molded itself to accommodate the crescent of her body. She burrowed deeper. Ready to sleep, she took one last deep breath, expelling it with a vague smile, when she felt something brush her cheek. She was about to lift her hand to her cheek when her body was lifted and turned, drawn forward by another body.

Kisses touched her face and neck, and hands slowly, sinuously moved up and down her body. No longer in her fetal position, her hands began to move, too, touching and feeling the lover next to her. It was a familiar figure, the arms muscular, the belly covered by smooth skin. Joyously, her hands confirmed David's presence and rapturously she kissed him, frantic now with happiness and reawakened senses. Only David could know those special places that heightened her senses and tantalized her, the satisfaction in the final abandonment of those senses. They came together, holding each other and feeling the tremors contorting their bodies.

Tired at last, they rested against each other, David's head on her breast. The sun dried the moisture from their bodies and warmed them, as they savored their sense of connection. But slowly a shadow covered them, and Diane looked up. Mark's face peered down at them, his eyes looking piercingly into hers.

She smiled at Mark, and he dropped down beside her. Uneasily, she looked at David, but his face revealed nothing. Gently, she lifted her arm from under him and shyly turned to Mark. He kissed her slowly, languorously. She touched his strange body, timidly at first and then more brazenly, intuitively aware of the pleasure her hands were generating.

Mark pulled her closer and then turned her around, his body over hers. The turn revealed David's face, and simultaneously a white-hot pain filled her chest with suffocating intensity.

She pulled herself away, shaking and sweaty, the couch no longer a carpet of grass but a narrow and confining bed. She lifted herself, tired and more depressed than ever. Her arm had been pushed up against the back of the couch, jutting the splint into her body. She hadn't hurt her arm, protected as it was. She lifted herself from the couch, a sense of fatigue making her feel more drained and depressed than before her nap.

She'd slept a long time, but it was still several hours before Stuart's visit. Perhaps a walk along Second Avenue or a movie might fill the time. Too tired for any of those activities, she settled for a game show on television. Her eyes focused on the screen for barely a minute. The sight of leaping, shrieking women fighting for the promise of money became so repugnant that she switched off the set. She turned the radio on and took up her book again. The phone rang. It was Allie.

Diane told her about the accident and was able to get her to agree not to tell Steve or the rest of the family. Allie was eager to see her. They made a date for the next night. Allie, though her sister-in-law, had become a dear friend. And now, even though Allie was separated from her brother, their relationship hadn't changed. In fact, it had improved. Allie was involved in her life in every way, almost like a mentor, like the sister she never had.

Allie was happy about her separation, but she was sorry about having children when she and Steve broke up. She wanted him to take them. She felt they tied her down. "I can't try my new wings with children there ready to clip them," she had said.

"You don't mean that, Allie," Diane replied, surprised and upset to hear those words.

"Of course, I love the kids. But what are they in for? Forget I said that. I don't know why I said that," she said almost apologetically. But Diane felt she meant it.

I'd never let David take the children. But there are no children to take. Allie loves the changes in her life. My changes frighten me.

Diane sat down again, the book tossed aside. She looked around the apartment, as if seeing it for the first time. Why, she wondered, had she committed herself to such an expensive apartment? Steve's friend Peter had the place before her and had mentioned he was leaving. Apartments in Manhattan were hard to find, almost impossible. She was one of the lucky ones. When she first saw it, she knew she had to have it. It was in an elegant building in a beautiful neighborhood—very chic. Peter had installed, on the advice of his decorator, pricey embellishments. Every room had been addressed, obviously sparing little expense. The bathroom had crystal faucets and beautiful tiles. The kitchen, too, had all kinds of improvements, like two stainless steel sinks, a small island for food preparation or snacking, and all sorts of handy gadgets plugged in and ready for use. But the bedroom was the best: the bed was raised on a platform and cabinets were tucked into the bottom of the bed. Lighting fixtures spanned the room, wrapping around the walls in a beautiful modern design. And when she saw it all, she knew she wanted to be in this place. She wanted to have something that would give her a fresh start, that would cheer her, and this apartment could do just that.

Of course, Peter said, he was aware that he couldn't expect to recoup all the costs of the improvements right away. He hoped, however, to see a substantial return, because, after all … and he went into another discourse on the attributes of the apartment and its current value, how it would be gone in a minute, and the only reason he let her see it was because of Steve. They settled on five thousand dollars for the renovations, which would be paid in monthly installments. Diane was elated to have gotten the apartment.

Now, six months later, the high cost of the apartment and the additional payments for the unnecessary ornamentation seemed like an albatross around her neck. She felt she might never be out of debt. Besides, cork-lined walls and crystal faucets didn't seem to matter anymore.

David had loved the apartment. The look on his face when he first saw it was partial compensation for its financial demands. She could even proclaim, with a certain amount of conviction, that her newfound independence hadn't left her bereft of resources. Overtly it mustn't matter that she hated the job, or that the monthly bills on the furnishings, rent, and utilities were compromising that sense of freedom, tying her to odious masters. It mustn't matter that she felt as though she had been set adrift in a turbulent sea, ill-equipped to battle the waves. What mattered was that David was impressed. She could see that from his eyes, scanning the rooms with appreciative glances.

I'd have gone back to the tiny flat downtown if he'd have just asked. It was homier and cozier than this empty showplace.

"Your job must be paying quite well," David had said admiringly.

"Oh, enough. I guess the important thing is that I like it so much. And, of course, I'm independent."

My other state never bothered me, though, perhaps because I never viewed myself as dependent. I just accepted our togetherness and the fact that your music provided for us. I'd gladly exchange this "independence" for the resumption of our former life.

She had been excited about showing him the apartment and seeing him again. They had kept in touch, seen each other occasionally; the separation had been friendly. But this visit was special, she thought. When she invited him to see the apartment, he seemed pleased. It seemed to be going well; they were both enjoying the wine, and David seemed to be enjoying the apartment. Then David got up and said he had to leave.

"But I thought you would have dinner here," she said.

"I'm sorry," he replied. "I didn't realize you were making dinner, and I made an appointment. Perhaps another time. I'll be in touch with you soon."

He kissed her cheek. She touched the edge of his lips. Then the door closed, and he was gone. The casserole in the oven dried to a straw-like texture while Diane cried.

Everyone had marveled at how well the divorce had gone. Even the lawyers who agitated for controversy were surprised at the lack of animosity, the complete accord. There was a small property settlement and an alimony arrangement. Diane at first refused to consider alimony but finally agreed to take a small monthly sum for a year and a lesser sum for the second year. After that, the payments would cease.

She and David continued to see each other, though the friendship naturally changed. Diane heard from friends about David's amorous adventures. They didn't mean to be hurtful; the information was leaked gratuitously, on rare occasions, but often she asked for it. She couldn't flinch from meeting old friends and pressed to hear new information. She almost felt as though it was a greater connection to David. Now that he was liberated from the confines of his marriage, he was savoring the delights of a single man—trotting from bed to bed, eager for the next foray into the unknown. At least, this was the way Diane interpreted the painful news.

Diane, however, fearful of her new independence, longed for the old and familiar world and found herself unable to respond to the overtures of interested admirers. Friends tried to introduce her to men but to no avail. Instead, she settled into a comfortable relationship with Stuart and a rather strained and difficult one with Michael, a man Steve had introduced to her.

Occasionally she would consent to see a stranger highly recommended by some well-meaning friend. The evening would invariably prove to be a dismal affair, her efforts at conversation difficult, her fear of physical contact inhibiting her innate warmth. She appeared cool and standoffish, hardly the promised enchantress her partner of the evening had expected to meet. Instead, he found a date who had retreated behind a cold stare and monosyllabic answers.

After the end of one of those tense evenings, she would ardently vow never again to allow herself to be persuaded to spend an evening with a stranger she was sure to find tiresome and repellent. Falling into the empty bed after such an evening would always arouse those wistful thoughts of David and the fun they had together, always ending the evening in each other's arms.

Weeks of sad lethargy followed, and she was again induced by a well-intentioned friend to be set up with another man. The silent and inevitable comparisons were made, and no, he didn't in any way resemble David. Another evening had been wasted in inane pleasantries and forced conversation, both parties finally relieved when the evening was over.

Surprisingly, it was Steve's introduction to Michael that evoked emotions of an earlier time. Michael was shy and unsure of himself; his gentle and subdued manner was touching.

The evening began like most others: there were awkward introductions at her door, rapid mutual appraisals, and meaningless amenities. Michael accepted her offer of a glass of wine and settled his large frame on the couch, listening with keen appreciation to David's music on the stereo, commenting, she remembered, on the sensitive interpretation of Chopin's music, while she poured him some red wine that had been opened just the day before. She set it down next to him.

"I'll be just a minute," she said as she went to the bedroom to finish dressing. She had gotten a late start that evening and, in addition to having to put the apartment in guest mode, had forgotten to change the CD. Rather than bring up a discussion about it, she'd pretended it was just another Chopin recording. When she was ready and came out of the bedroom, she saw the rapt expression on Michael's face, his total immersion in the romantic music that David was so capable of interpreting. She poured herself a glass of wine and sat down next to him.

They barely spoke a word, listening instead to the beautifully rendered sonata. The CD ended, and a Stravinsky work dropped into place. The juxtaposition of sound and melody made them laugh, and Diane switched off the CD, turning to a station of classical music.

"I'm afraid I got a bit carried away by the music," Michael started to apologize. "It was quite beautiful."

"It is, isn't it? It's my favorite recording, although I admire almost everything by Chopin."

"The interpretation, though, it was quite sensitive without being maudlin. You know, I should have gotten tickets for a concert. I think you'd have enjoyed that. Perhaps another time."

She filled their glasses with more wine, and she, too, leaned back into the sofa.

"Steve told me you work for an advertising agency. It must be fun. At least, less ponderous and discouraging than my work," Michael said.

"I think we're both wishing we were doing something else. I don't really like my job. In fact, I rather dislike it. It's dishonest, and I'm starting to feel it's a useless pursuit. People are competing to create needs, then fulfill the false needs they've created. You're doing something vital, something of real value."

"It's really rather discouraging, Diane. I remember when I was a resident, I was beginning to doubt the value of psychiatry and wondered what benefit was being served by my counsel. I was depressed then. I guess all these problems I had listened to were getting to me. I spoke to my chief—he must have known how I was feeling for some time. He didn't have any great suggestion or inspiring words for me. It would have been foolish to expect an easy solution, a panacea for my own self-doubts. 'Listen and prescribe the drugs that can make it easier for us to reach these people. Some we can cure, others, perhaps never, but we're trying. Besides, the meds are getting more effective,' was all he offered. I got some more encouragement, a little advice on how to remove myself from feeling so personally engaged with the conflicts I was listening to, but essentially, it came down to the fact that I've got to console myself with the little I can do. Small compensation, isn't it?"

Michael's honest uncertainty touched her. It was so unlike Steve's unquestioning confidence in himself and his craft. His colleagues and friends were of a similar mold, dogmatic in their opinions and seemingly unshakable in their belief in their own omnipotence. This man's doubt moved her. She had only known him for about a half hour, but she felt a kind of kinship with him. This sense of ease emboldened her to speak honestly with him.

"Why don't you change your specialty? Or is it too late?"

"I suppose because it was difficult enough to choose psychiatry. There wasn't much else I wanted to do."

Diane looked intently at Michael.

"You don't really like medicine, do you?"

"No, I guess not. Psychiatry seemed the most bloodless of the specialties, so I chose that. Then to compound my misery, I chose child psychiatry. I hoped that would offer a more positive view of the field's healing capabilities, but here, too, I'm discouraged. We're getting away from old theories, though. We're starting to question whether there isn't a physiological basis for mental illness, a genetic factor, perhaps, anatomical deviations … anomalies. We're treating the problems earlier; we're recognizing neurological disturbances." Suddenly Michael paused, as if he thought he may have been revealing too much of himself in their first meeting. "But why talk about that now? It's not very exciting conversation, is it?" he said, smiling almost sadly.

"What would you have really liked to do?" she asked, at once curious and strangely eager to know more about this self-effacing man.

"Well, if you promise not to laugh, I'll tell you." She nodded, giving the moment its due solemnity.

"I really wanted to be a concert pianist. I studied for several years and I loved it. Oh, I don't mean I was primed for a career in music. I took the usual once-a-week lessons and practiced whenever I had the time. There was school, and my grades were important. My folks had wanted me to enter medicine as early as I can remember. My father would bring home chemistry sets, and we'd concoct our own experiments. I actually enjoyed that. Then there was sports. Dad was a Yankee nut. I was a fairly active kid, played athletics well, studied hard, and tried to find time to play the piano. That was actually Mother's doing—the piano, I mean. She used to play a little, and she encouraged me, if one could say I needed the encouragement. She loved listening to me. I truly loved playing, but as I got older there seemed to be less and less time for practice. Finally, the lessons stopped, and I guess I just forgot about it. Just now and then I remember how I enjoyed the music and the effort. It was something I did for myself, without a return in any tangible sense ... just beautiful music ... " His voice trailed off in remembrance. "Say, are you hungry?" he asked, the revelations brought to a temporary halt.

"Yes, I am," she answered, for the first time in a long time looking forward to dining with another man.

They chose a small Italian restaurant in Gramercy Park. They ate and drank, fully enjoying their ample portions of wine, antipasto, warm, thick-crusted bread with olive oil, eggplant parmesan, lasagna, and a large bowl of pasta. The choice of dessert presented a formidable dilemma, as the abundant array of sweets made them greedy with childish delight. Laughingly, they proposed to share a dessert, and they chose tiramisu.

After dinner they walked along Third Avenue, talking and looking in shop windows. Eventually they tired and stopped at a small outdoor café for espressos.

They took a cab back to Diane's apartment, Diane moving to a neutral corner of the taxi, fearful now that any physical closeness might be misconstrued. They were silent, their gaiety replaced by a somber Diane plotting a gracious finale to the evening—almost hoping the plan would prove ineffectual. The problem, much to her confusion, was solved by Michael's quick departure after escorting her to her door and promising to call the following week.

Where had she heard that before? Obviously, the rapport she imagined they had shared was not enough to serve the end she was starting to envision. Relieved in one sense, Diane felt disappointed, too, because she did like him. Probably his friendship with Steve prompted him to appear interested. She must have been dull company, she thought. She readied herself for bed and decided to forget the evening.

Several days later, however, Michael phoned, asking to see her again. Surprised and pleased, she made a date for the following Saturday.

When the day arrived, she carefully examined her clothing, discarding almost everything she owned as dowdy or outmoded. Her previous disinterest in her looks was now replaced by a critical and minute examination of every part of her body.

She spent most of the morning exploring Joan's closet and finally decided on one of Joan's oversized filmy, white blouses, a brazenly bright pink cardigan with rhinestone buttons, and a pair of her own black tailored pants. She checked herself in the mirror regularly and spent the day grooming herself and the apartment. When evening finally arrived she was nervous and angry, vacillating between anticipation and overwhelming dismay at having made this date—and at the new and strange woman who stared back at her in the mirror.

To compound her misery, Michael was late, and she convinced herself that he had thought better of his request and simply decided not to appear. Much to her relief, the doorman rang up to announce his arrival, and a very apologetic Michael finally stood at the door, so sorry to have been so late. He had tickets to a concert, and if they didn't rush they'd be late. She grabbed a jacket, and both rushed to the elevator and then down to the avenue to get a taxi. In the cab, he seemed to want to further explain, but she hushed his apology; seeing him at last made the day's misgivings disintegrate. Besides, his diffident manner and attentiveness to her was starting to endear him.

After returning from a concert at the Lincoln Center and late dinner at a small Armenian restaurant, Michael seemed reluctant to leave her. The Chopin CD was playing and Diane had poured some red wine. They were on the sofa, Michael's head in her lap. They hardly talked; she ran her fingers through his hair, brushing his cheek with her hand. He reached up and brought her head down, kissing her. Then he lifted himself and took her in his arms, kissing her more fully. She stiffened, ending the kiss and turning her head away, but still holding on to him and feeling comfortable with his arms encircling her.

As if understanding her dilemma, he held her firmly, touching only her cheeks with his lips. They settled into a prone position on the couch, still holding each other but moving themselves to accommodate the curves and ridges of their bodies. They remained in one position for some time, finally peacefully dozing. Diane woke shortly, Michael's body stirring slightly. She snuggled closer to him, her face resting on his shoulder, her body half covering his.

Slowly her hand came around to the other side of his face, her leg drawing her body over his. She could feel herself almost covering him, the curves and hollows of his body fittingly meeting hers. Her hand explored his face and head; her lips moved to his lips, touching them slowly to her own. His hands began to rove over and down her back. He moved onto his side and then rolled over her, sliding his hand under her blouse, his hands more urgent than before. She stiffened again, resisting his hands and his body. Her hand caught his and brought it back around her waist. He sensed her fear; his hand lay quiet and steady where she had laid it.

"I'm sorry, Michael."

"Shh. I don't mind holding you like this, and besides, the anticipation makes it so much more delicious."

"You're not angry with me?"

"Of course not." He covered her face with soft kisses, his arms holding her closer.

"Why don't we go to your bed?" Michael proposed. Diane froze. "I could stretch my feet out. I promise not to touch you if you don't want that."

"You won't mind?" she murmured timidly.

"No."

She led the way through the dimly lit apartment, Michael holding her hand.

Sleepily, they fell onto the bed, quickly finding the most comfortable position within their embrace. They stayed that way for the next few hours, enjoying a good and deep sleep.

The early morning rays were coming into the shaded room, the soft lights of dawn giving the stillness a dreamlike quality. She looked into Michael's face, his person suddenly very dear, his kindness evinced by his patience and understanding. She wished this moment might last forever—the quiet room, the pale light, and Michael close in her arms. She moved even closer, wanting to awaken him and kiss his face, his lips set in an angelic pout, his dark, curly hair framing his peaceful features.

Diane stirred again, this time touching his neck. His eyes fluttered open, catching sight of her, and he brought his warm, sleepy face to her cheek. His body, wrapped around her, loose and pliant, felt like some protective shield, inuring her against unseen, unknown forces.

"Let's make love," she said, feeling free of some nameless burden.

"You're sure you want to? I can wait, you know."

"I want to," and with that reply she nuzzled closer, kissing his lips.

His body came alive, his hands moving to stroke and feel her and then remove the binding clothes. Finally they were both naked, Michael awed by her beauty. She came to him and hid herself, wrapping her arms around him. She was filled with a shyness she had not known since the first time David saw her nude. He, too, had admired the lush curves of her lithe, young form, and she found safety from her confusion and modesty in his arms, the way she did this morning.

Michael's hands moved along her hips and thighs, returning to the small but full breasts. He bent his head down and kissed her nipples, his hand moving down her pelvis. She ceased to think, her skin began to throb, and she felt herself start to open to meet the fullness of him. She felt him above her, straining his tense body to enter her. Her tingling excitation ceased; her eyes opened, focusing on Michael's reddened, sweat-filled face and rigid body contorted with painful exasperation, finally expelling great breaths and falling like a deadened mass on her breast. She held his wet head, brushing his hair and cheek with her hand in regular, constant motions.

Slowly, his breathing returned to normal, and then, the softer, less labored breath of sleep. Delicately, she extricated herself from under him, inching off the bed carefully so as not to wake him. She took a robe from the closet and went into the bathroom to shower. She made breakfast for herself and then went back into the bedroom, an instinct telling her that Michael would appreciate her presence when he woke. She stretched her body on the bed, careful to maintain a distance between herself and Michael; she didn't want to wake him yet.

How sad was the outcome of this first attempt at love—first, that is, since David. It was probably bound to be a failure from the very beginning. She didn't know how to stir a man; no doubt another woman would have prevented this fiasco, enabling them both to satisfy each other. It was possible that Michael was tired; after all, he had had very little sleep. A nagging voice at the back of her mind suggested that this problem might have nothing to do with her. And yet the doubts about her ability to excite him persisted, her overwhelming sense of failure resisting her efforts to blame him and not herself.

Later in the morning he woke. "What time is it?" he asked groggily.

"It's ten. Did you sleep well?"

"Yes."

"Would you like some juice?"

"I'd love some."

She brought him the juice, and he quickly finished it.

"I'd better get going," Michael said. "I've got to see someone about a car at twelve."

They both avoided mention of the incident. She went into the living room, and he dressed with haste. He kissed her quickly at the door and then disappeared down the corridor.

She went back into the living room, the bright October sun dappling the room with warm light. The plants looked thirsty. She took a pitcher to fill with water.

He must have been tired. That must be it. I kept him awake most of the night, and then he was too fatigued to be very active in lovemaking. I'll call him tomorrow, apologize for keeping him awake. The resolution pleased her and lifted her spirits.

The next day she called Michael as she had planned, but the apology froze in her mouth. He was glad to hear her voice. They moved easily into conversation, never broaching the awkward topic but still engaged and interested. He asked to see her next week. Gratefully, she said yes.

Her week was a bit more exciting now. She was looking forward to her date with Michael and anticipating an evening that had her wishing for its conclusion before its commencement. When the evening came, she was flushed and excited. She greeted him comfortably and warmly, determined to make all go well.

That evening's lovemaking proved as disastrous as their last attempt. Now Diane was forced to relinquish the blame for Michael's failure. His problem would have to be attributed to factors other than herself. Oddly, this knowledge made him dearer to her, and her attitude became gentler, more empathetic.

The fourth time they met, about a month later, Michael told her he was under analysis. He had concluded, over a long period of time and with the help of his analyst, that he could respond more positively if his partner were aggressive. Diane tried to become more aggressive, but her disinclination for the role somewhat inhibited her. A few times they succeeded, but it was always too hasty to be of any satisfaction to either of them.

By the end of three months, she was tiring of the situation and Michael. David's ebullience, on the rare occasions she saw him, seemed to intensify her own wretched state, though she outwardly maintained a cheerful and enthused air.

During this time, her friendship with Stuart had grown stronger.

He became her advisor and protector at work, and she became a maternal substitute of sorts—a personal confessor. New York was a long way from his native Iowa, and folks in Des Moines would not have been able to fathom the exploits of their quiet, blue-eyed darling. She listened to his disappointments and relished his joys, vicariously thrilling to each new romantic episode, as though her contribution was her own desire to love and be loved. Often Stuart took her to parties, introducing her to another side of New York she had never known. It was no longer the straight world, filled with familiar conventions, but a freer though often more desperate world, sometimes drugs alleviating the pain in that world.

Eventually the parties began to bore her, the conversations all too often meaningless and vapid, and the raucous music dissonant, like the intrusive thoughts of her mind. More and more she was dwelling on her past life and the togetherness and serenity she shared with David.

Her dissatisfaction in her relationship with Michael prompted her to discontinue seeing him, but his sad persistence made it a difficult and futile task. She didn't want to cause him pain.

Diane's disinterest at her job grew steadily; her unanticipated quasi promotion as an assistant account manager was a meaningless reward. She was saddled with bills, and the extra work didn't bring with it more money. It didn't change anything except give her more responsibility. The apartment seemed large and joyless, and she envisioned a life of lonely decline. She started to dream of death, going so far as to pretend the night's sleep was death coming to claim her. The mornings became desperate battles to leave the bed, her energy seemingly sapped during the heavy sleep. She'd lie in the bed, promising herself only another five minutes of sleep but dozing off for fifteen. The hated office waited; the bills seemed to mount while she tarried under the covers.

She began to dream of her funeral, always noticing how sad David was in the scenes at the cemetery. The eulogy was always brief. There was very little to say about her achievements or contributions to society. One couldn't proclaim to the assembly, "She gave us a fine piece of copy for the soap to end body odor," or, "How about that commercial for wart medicine!" No, it didn't quite fit.

But at the cemetery, when all the words had been spoken and the only act left was the lowering of the coffin, she could see David's face, desperately straining to keep the tears from coming, finally giving way to the grief that shook his body.

He might even have wished he'd acted differently, but it would be too late. He'd grieve for a short time, but there would be too many willing friends ready to help assuage his grief. Still, the image of a grieving David, even betraying a short-lived sorrow, gave her some comfort.

Her bleak outlook continued for many weeks. She lost count of how many. She began to tire easily and looked forward to sleep, as if that were the panacea for every problem she faced. Maybe the sleep would give her energy for tomorrow; maybe the sleep would obliterate today. Once in bed, she'd close her eyes and try to imagine the nothingness of death, only to have an image of David or Michael appear before her.

Finally, she made this failed attempt at ending it all. It changed little in her life except for making ordinary things enormously difficult, albeit temporarily. Nothing had really changed. The job was hers when she was well enough to return, Michael would be calling soon, and Stuart would arrive this evening, bubbly and full of tales of his lively weekend with his lover of the week.

Chapter 5

As though her thoughts of Stuart were the cue for his arrival, the bell rang and she answered it, dreading the inevitable questions.

"Oh dear, it looks much worse than I suspected," Stuart began, staring at her bandaged hands.

"It's not really so bad, so don't get so upset. What did you bring to eat? I'm starved," she said with as much enthusiasm as she could muster.

"Let's see. I've got egg drop soup, lo mein, egg rolls, and spareribs. Will you be able to manage?" he said, looking again at her hands, the fingers barely poking out.

"Of course, you'll just have to play host and get the dishes from the kitchen."

"First, tell me how you're feeling." Sincere concern for his friend was evident in his voice.

"I'm fine. Really. The bandages are coming off in a couple of days, and I'll be back to work by the end of the week." She smiled, trying to look perky, as though this trivial matter was light and inconsequential.

"That's good to know. You've been missed. Hal's been a bear, especially since we lost the Gracey account. And on top of that he's had his budget trimmed. There's no living with him at the moment.

"Please, Stu, let's not talk about the office."

"You're still down on it, aren't you?"

"It only seems to get worse. I'm wondering what I'm doing there now. Why I stay. I hate the lies. I couldn't care less about whiter teeth and fresher breath, or blue water in my toilet bowl. It has absolutely no meaning for me. I can't even watch a television commercial without becoming upset. Lies—that's all we're feeding them, and for what purpose? To make more money for an account and then have the account leave in the hopes that another agency can do even better? Everyone is constantly on the alert, fearful of losing their jobs, ready to turn their mothers in for some inside dope." Her voice was rising; she was venting her anger, out of frustration and her sense of failure. She continued, her voice still raised but the anger ebbing. "I think it's the strategy of the account exec. I think it's something to make us all turn against each other."

"Aren't you being a little hard on the agency? You know, Hal's been very pleased with your work."

"Oh, Stu, I don't care what Hal thinks. I have to wonder what I'm doing, what the work means to me. I can't find any rationale for spending eight, ten hours a day or more, five days a week in that place. It's starting to stink of lies, intrigues, and gross deceit. Haven't you felt that way about it? No, I suppose not. You sit in your cubicle, design clever layouts for the consumer's visual appreciation or deception, and … "

Diane looked at Stuart's face, seeing the hurt in his eyes, and she stopped herself.

"I'm sorry, Stu. I guess I'm down and I'm taking it out on the job … and you, because you remind me of it. Let's eat."

She followed him into the kitchen and directed him to the proper utensils. His apparent glumness after his exuberant entry made her feel guilty. She determined to cheer him or at least amend the earlier aura of her despair and her angry outburst. He'd come over to help her, cheer her, and here she was trashing him. She'd soothe him; she could do that.

"How was your weekend?" Diane began brightly. "Tell me what you did."

"Actually, this weekend was probably my quietest in a long time. I was exhausted from last week, if you remember, so I decided to take it easy. Saw a lovely film, De Sica's last, as a matter of fact. It was quite good. Went with Fred. You remember, I told you about him. He's working in the chorus of *Rent*. Not terribly interesting, but better than nothing."

Diane saw something shift in his expression, and she could tell that he was back to himself again, enthused about being her center of attention.

"Sunday I lounged around. I called you, as a matter of fact. Thought you might like to go to the Met. They're having an exhibit of Oriental art. You weren't home—or at least you weren't answering." Stuart eyed her with a questioning glance. Diane remained silent. "We can make it some other time, I suppose. Another friend called, and we went to a rug auction at the Carlton."

Just then the phone rang and Diane excused herself. It was Michael.

"I can't talk long. I have company now."

"I just called to … can I see you this weekend? Carol, my friend Richard's wife, you remember her, don't you? Well, she invited us out to the house for the weekend. The ride out to the country would be so nice. The leaves are turning. It must be beautiful."

He's straining. Hoping I'll consent. "All right."

"I'll pick you up about ten." The phone clicked off.

When she returned to the table, Stuart was furiously twisting his lo mein around his fork, having finished his soup.

"How am I going to manage this, I wonder," she said.

"Why don't we cut it into little pieces? I'm sorry. I guess I wasn't thinking when I ordered."

"Don't be silly. I love lo mein. I'll just do as you say. Oh, I forgot, there's some wine in the fridge, if you want."

"Haven't had wine with Chinese food in a long time. Let's try some."

The wine seemed to raise Stuart's spirits. His natural effervescence now seemed to grate on her nerves. She was starting to tire and longed to be alone.

The phone rang again. This time she took the call in the bedroom. Pat, another friend who lived in the building, was distraught after learning of Diane's accident from Joan.

"I'm fine. You'll see for yourself," Diane assured her.

I could invite her up. Then Stu wouldn't be alone with me, and they could amuse each other.

"Pat, would you like to come up? My friend Stu is here. You could join us for dinner."

"I wouldn't want to intrude."

"I'd love to see you, and we have plenty of food. More than enough—I seem to have lost my appetite. Please come up."

"You're sure you won't mind?"

"I give you my word."

"I'll see you in a few minutes."

More likely a half hour, Diane thought. *Hearing a male is here can only mean to Pat a chance at another date. She'll put her best face forward, no matter how long it takes to paint on. I'm being vicious. Oh, it doesn't matter—she can't hear. What's wrong with me? What's happening to me? Why didn't I tell her Stu was gay? Because I don't tell people who's gay and who's straight. But she'll think he's a potential lover. I don't care.*

Diane remained in the bedroom for a few minutes, sitting alone on the badly made bed. She didn't want to see Stu yet. It was almost as though she were afraid he'd read her thoughts.

"Di, is everything all right?" he called.

She walked out of the bedroom. "I hope you don't mind, Stu. A friend called and I invited her up. She just heard about my accident and wanted to see me. You don't mind, do you?"

"Of course not," he said. But she could tell he did.

"She probably won't stay long. I'm sorry, Stu, I'm not very good company tonight." *Why am I apologizing now? All I can think of is that I am completely, utterly exhausted.*

"Poor baby," he said. "Does David know about what happened to you?"

"He's away on tour in South America again. Besides, I wouldn't tell him. He has his own life. Let's not talk about him, please."

The doorbell saved her from the tears that were threatening to start. Gratefully, she opened the door for Pat, who was visibly distressed at the sight of her friend's bandaged hands. "What happened?" she exclaimed with real concern in her voice, her face tight with unnamed fear.

"It's all coming off Wednesday. It doesn't hurt, and I'm feeling fine. Now sit down and join us for some dinner. You don't know Stu, do you?" she said, trying to keep things light and minimize Pat's dismay … or was it fear?

She introduced them, wondering when Pat would discover that Stu would have no romantic interest in her and wishing that she would have said something in advance of the meeting.

"Stu, would you mind getting Pat a plate and glass?"

"Done."

"Tell me how this happened, Diane. Joan said you fell in the living room."

"That's all that happened. Really. Now it's healing." *Another explanation and I'll do it again.*

Stu came in with the dinnerware, and he filled Pat's plate with lo mein and ribs and poured some red wine for her. Diane's usually hardy appetite had been flagging of late. In fact, she hardly thought of food. It was a welcome consequence of her depression. She might even manage to lose a few pounds.

Diane's two friends seemed perfect dinner partners, both of them eating voraciously, taking time out now and then to laugh at some inanity. The sounds of eating and laughter in the apartment were troubling her. It was as though she were invaded by the outside world, and the quiet, dreamy one she inhabited was being violated.

They'll be gone soon. And at least I'm not boring Stu or making him uncomfortable with my diatribes against a profession he admires. I'd started to deprecate his work. But he loves what he does and is probably the only one who brings some beauty to the lie, making it more palatable for all of us. But couldn't he use his artistic talent to the benefit of other causes and earn a living in the process? Oh, eat your egg roll and leave Stu alone. He's happy. Or is he?

"Diane, can you pass the rice?" said Stu, interrupting her thoughts. "Oh, sorry," he said right after his question.

"I've got it," Pat said, and then made some other remark that made Stu laugh. Diane didn't even note it. She kept slowly chewing the small amount of food in her mouth, still thinking of Stu and his life.

He runs so fast from one event to another, or one party to another. I wonder if he has the time to assess his life, and if he does, what judgment he makes. He gives and takes love, if I can call it that, on the run, rarely committing himself to any long-term relationship. Tells me monogamy is a male-female hang-up, jealousy too. All the inhibitors to freedom and sensual pleasures. Possession can never imply love anymore than marriage means compatibility. These are obsolete values, he says, that no longer serve any function. Male possessiveness was only to insure rights of progeny; female possessiveness was a backlash of the demands of virginity or "virtue." But why am I obsessing on this stuff right now? I should be playing a better host, even though having these people here right now is making me want to scream.

"Diane, do you like that egg roll?" Stu asked. "You've hardly touched it."

"No, it's delicious. I'm just eating slowly," she said, trying to sound enthused but annoyed at the interruption of her thoughts.

"Well, you've hardly touched it."

"I'm working on the lo mein," she said, poking her fork at that dish to show her intent. Pat and Stu went on about some other issue, and she resumed her thoughts.

He really cares about me, I know that. But I don't agree with his ideas. There's more to love than possession and jealousy. Maybe it boils down to self-serving interests in its most basic form, but it's a caring and serving that can benefit the loved one. David's happiness was mine. I gloried in his achievements because they reflected on me. Maybe I was nothing without David—maybe his love was my only reason to exist. Maybe you're right, Stu, but how many bodies must you have and when do you reach that pinnacle of pleasure? What pleasure anyway? What am I thinking about?

"Diane, you're really not eating. What's wrong?" Stu asked.

"Nothing, I'm just not hungry."

"Just look at what's going to be left over," said Pat, the daytime social worker voicing her work mentality.

"Pat, anything I eat now will definitely not aid an Indian or African child. If I thought it would, I'd lick my plate. And, anyhow, look how fat everyone's getting."

"I don't know. I can't throw food away anymore. It makes me feel so guilty, knowing people are starving and I'm discarding food."

"But your consumption of food doesn't change the situation one iota," Diane persisted. "Besides, think of the food your little dog, Tara, consumes. One can of those beef chunks would feed a hungry child for a week ... well, maybe a few days."

"I suppose you're right, but if you really don't want anymore, Stu and I will finish it. This food is delicious."

Pat divided the remaining portions, adding a little to Diane's plate, ignoring her feeble protestations.

"Have a little more wine, Diane. It will perk you up."

"It's just making me sleepy tonight. I'd better not."

"Well, you don't have far to go if you need to go to sleep," said Stu with a smile.

"Thanks, but I don't think so," she said with finality.

"Okay, we'll kill the bottle then," he said, pouring the remains for himself and Pat.

The sounds of eating, the tinkling of silver on china, even the rustling of the napkins were annoying Diane.

"If you guys don't mind, I'm going to sit on the couch for a few minutes. I'm getting tired," she said, with evident fatigue and a trace of irritation.

"You go right ahead and rest," said Pat. I'll clear the table and stack the dishes. You can turn on the dishwasher whenever you want."

"I'll clear the table, really. Just leave the things," said Diane with little conviction.

"Nothing doing. I'm the chief dishwasher tonight," said Pat with mock brightness.

"Then, I'm the chief's assistant," said Stu with his own brand of brightness.

This banter, too jolly for Diane, sent her silently to the couch, glad to be able to sit alone and think while her friends amused themselves.

They cleared the table amidst a clatter of glasses, plates, spoons, forks, and never-ending chatter. Then they joined her, ostensibly to cheer her. *Surely they'd prefer to leave*, Diane thought, *but a sense of duty must be compelling them to stay.*

"Look, why don't you guys play backgammon? You know where the set is, Pat. And I know you love to play, Stu.

"That's the best idea you've had all day, my friend," said Stu.

Pat got out the set and the two of them became immersed in the game. Diane put some French music on the stereo, the wailing tones of Piaf greeted with boos from her small audience.

"Don't you have something really good, like U2 or even Sinatra? Anything but that," said Stu, still eyeing the dice and debating his move.

"Sorry, would you prefer something classical? No, I guess not. Wait, how about flamenco music. I've got something really good—Carlos Montoya."

She sifted through her CDs and found one she wanted. Delicately balancing the thin disc between her fingers, she placed it in the portal. Soon the guitar was sobbing its Moorish lament, after a short, spirited introduction. By now, Stu and Pat were so involved in the game that the guitar was of no consequence to them, but for Diane the music conjured up pictures of Spain and friendly people with wide, welcoming smiles on warmly tanned faces.

She and David had once rented a small house in Marbella, on the southern coast of Spain, close to the water and lonely enough to be claimed as their domain. Each morning, David would practice while she would go to the village and purchase the day's food requirements. In the afternoon, David would join her for a swim on the beach. On evenings that they wanted diversion, they would ride into Málaga for a hearty paella dinner and later visit a café to hear Andalusian music. The guitars never failed to stir her, the demanding texture of finger on string evoking an earthy response, an elemental passion.

The dancers enhanced the music, interpreting the beckoning sounds with eloquence. Lightly, then more imperiously, their feet would come alive, their hands goading them on in rapid clicks of the castanets. The dancers' bodies, no longer curved and pliable, would stiffen, and they would throw their hands back and begin to tempt, tall and proud. Oblivious now to all externals, the dancers would progress from slow taps of their feet to hard, rhythmic thrusts into the ground. Faster and faster their feet went, till her eyes were mesmerized by the stamping legs, jabbing and lashing with almost superhuman propulsion. Finally, the dancers' energy spent, they would slow the speed, their arms uplifted and their heads falling to their chests, their bodies still rigid from exertion but exhilarated by the final dramatic thrust of their feet and hands. The dancers would stand immobile, like magnificent statues, newly sculpted. Then slowly they would come to life, bowing with regal grace.

The scene never failed to awe her, though David was less impressed. But there was little that could make David ecstatic, she thought. His moments of elation seemed confined to those notes he drew out of his instrument, to the quiet joy he knew when a piece had been played particularly well and his audience rejoiced. A good meal pleased him, travel and new faces pleased him, but he reserved his joy for his keyboard. This was where he spoke and received the answer he desired, where he could transpose his thoughts into a substance no longer tangible but far more splendorous than anything else he could imagine. He could not even attempt to separate the music from his body or the impulses that created it. He was joined in the music by the sheer force of the will to create the most beautiful expression of his being, and this was what she knew of him. She knew she was apart from him when he was involved with his music, but she knew he was hers when they shared their lovemaking.

David was, nevertheless, always amused by his wife's enthusiasm for most art forms. Hadn't he laughingly told her that she couldn't see a wall with free space without putting a painting or photograph on it? Sometimes the artist would become a friend, giving the object a history or genealogy, and she knew, without David saying a word, that he appreciated it.

Dance was Diane's favorite art form. Until her discovery of flamenco, classical ballet had claimed her loyalty. David lacked any great interest in the dance, so they didn't frequent the ballet; but he could tell those times were very special to Diane, who watched every movement with rapt attention, while he could appraise the music and its relationship to the action on stage.

Watching the flamenco dancers, she had that same rapt look, only more intense, as though she had discovered some ultimate truth within the confines of the café. This distance in thought, her surrender to the dancers, frightened him—she sensed that. After a glass of sherry in the now quieted cafe, she'd unwind and return to him in the way he understood. He seemed not to connect to her at those times, and she knew he needed to have her emotionally, always.

Sometimes after watching the dancers she'd feel more desirable, and her lovemaking would be more passionate and far more aggressive than usual. David likened her response to the nights he played a concert. She knew he'd need her later, when the well-wishers had left his dressing room, when he'd consumed a feast prepared in his favorite restaurant, and when they were home at last, still exhilarated but alone with their triumph. Then he could loose his yet unsated desire, and her willing body was there to receive him.

The music in Diane's apartment ended, but the silence didn't seem to affect the players. Pat and Stu were still deeply involved in their game, while Diane was remembering Granada, Seville, and the sun-whitened houses on the beach in Marbella.

"That's it, I've won," laughed Stuart victoriously.

"C'mon, Diane, join us in a card game. How about hearts or whist?" asked Stu.

"All right. I'll get the cards."

She brought out a deck of cards, and they cleared the table. They chose to play hearts because the game could go fast and amuse easily. Her guests seemed to enjoy this more than backgammon, but she felt little enthusiasm for it. It was difficult for her to hold the cards, and though she played well, she cared little about her score. Besides, it was getting late and she was tired.

Suddenly, Pat was laughing. "I've got them all!" she shrieked. "Queen and all."

"Twenty-six points to us both," said Stuart, looking at Diane. She was tired, stifling a yawn and very uncaring about her twenty-six penalizing points. He noticed her disinterest and fatigue and suggested they end the game. She didn't resist and they collected the cards, Pat putting things in order.

"I'm sorry I've been such bad company," Diane apologized.

"We've enjoyed ourselves, haven't we, Pat?"

"Definitely. We'll have to do this again some time."

"Yes, we will get together again. Just as soon as I can entertain properly." *It didn't matter whether I was here or not*, she thought. *The two of them hit it off so well, thank goodness.*

"I'll call you tomorrow," Stuart told Diane, kissing her on the cheek.

"Thanks for dinner. I really did appreciate it."

"You hardly ate anything."

"I probably wouldn't have eaten anything at all if you hadn't come."

Pat lingered in the kitchen, putting more things away and then coming out to say good-bye to Stuart.

The apartment quieted down with Stuart's departure. He seemed to emit waves of nervous energy that made any enclosure too small for his frantic movements. Pat, at least, was a more sedate companion.

"Well, I guess I'll be going. Everything's in order in the kitchen."

"Sit for a while," Diane insisted. "I have a feeling you'd like to talk."

"But you're tired. I can tell."

"No, really. I'm feeling better. Why don't you make some coffee and we'll relax?"

Diane could sense Pat's need to tell her about John and her newest conflict in her attempt to make him marry her. Tired as she was, she didn't have the heart to let her go without talking about it. It was all they seemed to have in common—their men and their disappointments.

"Does David know about your accident?"

"No, he's in South America. He won't be home for a couple of weeks. Besides, I don't think I would have told him. I'm trying to wean myself away from him. This certainly wouldn't help."

"Have you seen John recently?"

"I saw him this weekend. We had the same argument and, as usual, nothing was resolved." She sighed heavily, picked on an imaginary piece of hair or lint on her sweater, and looked wearily at her friend.

Diane thought a while before she decided to come to the point. She was too tired to be gentle now, too dull for diplomacy.

"Pat, why don't you stop trying to make him marry you and simply accept the relationship as it is?"

"Because if he really loves me as he says he does, then I can't understand why he would refuse to marry me. At this point, I don't know if I want to keep seeing him or not. We had a battle royal Saturday night. We were in a restaurant with several other couples. He took the number of one of the girls. I was furious, but he couldn't understand why. I don't know why I see him. He does such spiteful things and then tells me he loves me and needs me. I don't know what to do." Pat was trying to contain her tears but couldn't. She sobbed and grabbed a napkin, dabbing at her eyes.

"Perhaps if you didn't push him he'd come around on his own accord."

"If I thought that would work I'd try it, but he would never even have brought up marriage if I hadn't broached it first," Pat said rapidly, trying to hold back the tears and finally succeeding.

"Pat, you're going to be angry with me, but I think I've got to say this. I'm starting to feel that marriage may only benefit us ... women." At the startled look on her friend's face, Diane qualified her statement.

"Before you jump on me, listen. John's been married before. He has an ex he'll be paying alimony to for the rest of his life—presumably she'll outlive him—and children he loves. He's free to date whomever he pleases and maintain a relationship for as long as he pleases with or without emotional or financial commitment. Why in heaven's name should he want to marry? It could only be to satisfy your wishes. He can't really attain some heretofore unknown state of bliss. All right, I'm exaggerating, but really, the reason, the only reason, he could have for marrying you is to make you more secure—and why must the responsibility of your emotional health be placed on his shoulders?"

"He could also want to marry me ... just because ... because if you love someone you want to please that person."

"Then please him too. Don't tie him down with a piece of paper."

"But I want children. I'm getting older. I'm not going to be able to bear children much longer." This time Pat's voice was pleading, as though the verbalization of the fact might bring her wishes to fruition, might fulfill the terrible longing gnawing at her insides.

"You want a baby badly. How about having one without being married? You're a social worker. You have a good salary. Your field is pretty secure. What's to stop you?" Diane spoke faster than usual, expecting a certain amount of shocked dismay from her friend. Instead, she was surprised when Pat replied rather pensively that she'd thought about it.

"I guess I'm just not radical enough to do it. I'd have to hassle my family, no easy task if you knew them, religion and all. And then there'd be other problems, my own, I guess. I'd feel as though I was scorning conventions, rebelling against established mores, when in reality I'm not a terribly rebellious person, not really rebellious at all. If anything, I'm rather conservative.

"I'm not against the idea, though. As I said, I thought about it, only I'm not an innovator. I want an ordinary, conventional life with John. I want my children to know and love their father, and I want the security of knowing a man is protecting us. I can't change those feelings. Maybe if I had been brought up differently, I might be more courageous, but I have to accept this is the way I feel."

"Of course. You're right. You know yourself best. It just bothers me to see you hurt by John, though I'm sure he's isn't hurting you intentionally."

"No, I don't think he is either."

After a pause, Pat asked, "What about you and David? Didn't you want children?"

"Oh, I did, but he didn't. Sometimes I'm sorry we didn't have any, and other times I guess I'm glad they're not here. It's sort of like my imaginary children are spared my pain. Selfishly, I'd love to have children. I kind of envy Joan and the fact that she isn't so alone, but I couldn't offer my children very much, at least not now. David was my world, and when he left ... I guess, when I left him, it was like my foundations were pulled from under me." Her voice lowered, the words slowed. She got up and walked into the kitchen to wipe at some imaginary spots on the stove.

"But you came together again, didn't you?" said Pat, following behind.

"For a short time," she answered, going back to the living room and pouring herself some more coffee. She sat down with the cup held in her two hands and sipped slowly. Then she said, almost as though she were talking to herself, "When we got together again, it was as though David felt he couldn't live without me. For about a month we were deliriously happy." Her voice rose with the memory. "I determined never again to think disloyal thoughts or ever displease David in any way. I don't think we had ever been so happy."

In a softer, slower voice she said, "Everything just went so well …" Her voice trailed off. When she resumed she spoke in a low voice, almost void of feeling, almost as though she was stating a fact. "That level of contentment can be hard to sustain. Maybe that was the real problem. We could never again just relax into the essence … the plain, simple satisfaction of our relationship, and accept that some problems would be perfectly normal." She stopped again and took a sip of the coffee.

Pat waited.

She began again, stronger than before, as though she were shaking off the memory of the previous sentence. "David started to become restless this time. The whole thing just disintegrated. After that, we, or I, just longed for what had been." She took another sip of the coffee and quieted herself again. She rested her head against the back of the couch.

"But, you do see him, don't you?" Pat asked.

"Yes, pretty often. He seems to be enjoying his life, though sometimes I think he's waiting for another word from me to come back. I don't know if that's my imagination or it's a fact. I'm scared," she admitted and seemed more alert, poised for some imagined action. "If I make an overture and he rejects it, I'll hate myself and think that he'll become disgusted with me. If I don't do anything, I'll always wonder what might have been." She sighed again and took another drink.

"I wish someone would just come into my life and sweep me off my feet and help me forget him. Not even give me time to wonder. Then I'd forget David and my old life. But that's not going to happen, is it?"

Pat refilled her cup, and Diane thought that Pat must be thinking it wouldn't be a bad solution for her either.

"I don't know if he's still living with Elizabeth, but I'm going to start hoping we can get together again." Her voice rose, as though the words were giving her strength. "I haven't done that in a while. I'm going to hope and work for that." Diane laughed. "You know, I'm doing exactly what I told you not to do."

Chapter 6

THE NEXT MORNING DIANE VENTURED OUT OF her apartment to the lobby for the mail. Opening the mailbox with the thin key was difficult, and she was glad that only the doorman was in the lobby. Her mail had accumulated, and she could see a card from David in the middle of a pile of bills. "The tour has been going well," he wrote. He continued that he would vacation for a week in Brazil and be home in about two weeks. He looked forward to seeing her.

Her spirits soared; the day seemed alive with promise and hope. The bright October sunshine dazzled her eyes, the fallen leaves rustling musically near the open glass doors of the apartment house. It was a beautiful day. She looked out at the street, which was now filled with a life and color she hadn't noticed before. She bundled her mail in her arms and rode the elevator to her floor. It was important to leave this apartment-turned-prison, get some fresh air, and join the world again, because life had suddenly become dear and precious, and she was grateful to be alive and waiting for David. She found a light jacket and was able to put it on. She thought with relief that the splints were almost invisible—and so were the scars of her mind this morning.

She walked toward Second Avenue, the rush of working people gone but a brisk traffic still parading down the avenue. She stared at shop windows, looking at everything as though it were the first time she had seen the displayed items. She drank in the crisp warmth of the sun and the light it was casting on every object. The noises of activity and movement were almost musical, an urban symphony, dissonant and disconnected, but subliminally stimulating.

A new resolve had taken root in her mind last night. Even as she spoke to Pat of the futility of forcing John to marry her, she began to envision a reconciliation between her and David. True, David professed to like his newfound freedom, but she could tell he was lonely, that he seemed to need her and still want her as he had before. It was just possible that another chance for getting together as a loving couple was just two weeks away. Hope, and the conviction of her thoughts, started giving her a new outlook, and it was changing her mood.

That first reconciliation, she thought, was too soon after the separation. It was as though a connecting wire was broken and the repair too hastily attempted. The connection was weak. Neither of them faced reality but brushed it aside, too absorbed in the mere joy of being together again.

She walked into the supermarket and browsed through the shelves, wanting to buy a treat for herself and her sister-in-law tonight. Perhaps a rich and creamy Brie or Camembert on French bread with a red wine. She left the market and headed uptown for the cheese shop. She picked a ripe Brie, a large wedge of Gouda, some Danish blue cheese, and a baguette, a salesman helping her remove her money and placing the bag in her hands. She took the package home and placed the cheese on the table so it would be rich and creamy by tonight. Then she went to the liquor store to choose a good wine. By this time it was two o'clock and she was starting to feel hungry—a first since her "accident." She'd pick up a sandwich after buying her wine. She chose an expensive wine, laughing as the clerk tried to find the best position for her to carry the somewhat cumbersome bottle. She had only a short distance to walk, so its weight didn't really bother her.

Upon her return, the doorman informed her that Joan had been looking for her. He offered to buzz her and let her know that Diane had arrived. "And, how are your hands feeling?" he inquired.

"Well," she said, "and thank you for asking."

The lobby was full with afternoon traffic. Children were coming home from school and women were returning from errands. She smiled at the children and they returned her greeting, then quizzically stared at her hands. A few familiar faces looked alarmed when they saw her; others were merely curious. She allayed their concern with a cheery smile, newly practiced, and the accompanying statement that "it looks worse than it is." Mercifully, the elevator arrived and the conversations came to a halt.

When Joan telephoned later, Diane invited her up.

"I can't come yet. I have to wait for Melinda and Jason to come home from school. They should be here in about half an hour. I'll see you then."

Good, Diane thought. She had forgotten to get the sandwich, so she foraged through the fridge and grabbed something to eat. She found some leftovers and hungrily tore into them. It was a rather strange feeling to be home on a weekday, eating lunch at 2:30, waking after 9:00. In just a few days she'd forgotten what it was like not to have to meet schedules. She also supposed she might not like too much more of that sort of situation, at least not without David to make the day interesting.

As she was eating, the bell rang. She walked to the door, forgetting her hunger and thinking she'd be glad to see Joan. Instead, Ellen, a casual acquaintance from the apartment down the hall, greeted her. She was a divorced woman with two grown children who were married and seemed uncaring of their mother. Diane knew this because often Ellen would ask her in and complain about her children. Diane sensed she needed people to fill the emptiness of her time. Her loneliness was a discomfort to everyone who met her. Her silent plea for companionship often went unheeded; she was bitter and lost few opportunities to vent on whomever might be unfortunate enough to be within hearing distance. Ellen's days were empty and sad.

Ellen's life as the wife of an affluent and respected member of the financial community had ended in a bitter divorce, after an angry, venomous separation. Luckily, she would say, recounting those times, she had gone into analysis just two years before. She became aware of strengths she had never known she possessed. And she had become aware of those weaknesses that had dominated her life. Concurrently, her marriage began to change. It was the changing times and values, her new sense of worth, that were wreaking their havoc on her husband and the foundations of her marriage. It finally collapsed, but luckily, she would say again, the analyst was there to comfort and help her find her strength to begin a new life.

The lawyers put together a settlement that gave her a monthly income far less than she had anticipated. To conserve what she considered her paltry payoff, she moved into Diane's apartment house. To supplement her income, but more important, to fill her days, she would occasionally do substitute teaching. Those times didn't come very often, so she began to consider other kinds of employment. After several attempts to enter the job market and receiving only rejections in return for her efforts, she decided to concentrate on her teaching, whenever the opportunity might occur. Several times Diane had suggested she return to college, perhaps work toward a master's or even switch fields entirely, but this was impractical, Ellen would say.

"But you have such lovely taste in decorating and art," Diane insisted. "You could go to design school, begin a career in decorating or something related to that field."

"What nonsense. I'd have to start at the bottom, probably an errand girl of some sort. Besides, who would hire a fifty-year-old woman?"

"You certainly don't look fifty, and why do you think you'd necessarily start at the bottom?"

"Because in this world it's who you know, not what you know. All right, maybe if I were a society matron, someone might be interested in my decorating skills, want to use my name, but I'm just a fifty-year-old woman with a degree in education and few qualifications for anything else. Right now the market is glutted with teachers, so it doesn't even help to have a degree in education."

Once, Diane had suggested Ellen adopt an orphan; after all, she did have an extra room and her time was hardly filled. Though Ellen considered her alimony check small, and certainly it was a restrictive amount in view of her former wealth, it was still a handsome sum. Surely a young refugee from some current war zone or famine-ravaged country would be grateful for a home and some attention. Ellen wouldn't hear of this; her days of child-rearing were finished, she insisted. Her ungrateful children had given little in return for her caring and love.

There was little Diane could say in rebuttal. She was saddened by this woman's plight, by the complete upheaval of her former life, but she felt Ellen's sense of hopelessness reaching out into her, making her view her life, or her aspect as a female, in a strange, discomforting way. Ellen's hatred of men was overwhelming, her scorn for society only equaled by her scorn for its institutions.

Diane started avoiding her. Ellen's harangues against almost everything she touched upon were wearing Diane down. Her bitterness was frightening, a prophecy, perhaps, of Diane and her friends in another ten years. Maybe there were just too many disillusioned and lonely women haunting the world. But now, Ellen's presence at the door was an unwelcome distraction. *Where,* she wondered, *was Joan?*

"Ellen, hi," she said, with little else to guide the conversation. "Is everything okay?"

"I'm fine. I was just wondering what had happened to you. I heard from a neighbor you were hurt. I was wondering if I could help you."

"Thanks, Ellen. I'm really fine and my friend Joan will be here in a few minutes. Would you like to come in?" she asked, just to be polite. Could she really take Ellen now, she wondered?

"No, thanks. As long as you have a friend coming by, I'll come another time. Take care," Ellen said and walked back to her apartment.

Sort of strange, Ellen refusing the invitation, Diane thought. But maybe she had her reasons. It really didn't matter. Nothing much mattered now except the growing concept of her and David returning to their former life. Still, Ellen's presence left her with a chill in her being. She was back to thinking how romance could sour so easily, as happened with her and David. Why, even watching two cinema lovers walking into the sunset no longer presented a concept of everlasting happiness; it could only be a brief but beautiful encounter. Instead, it was that lone individual finding self-fulfillment and personal truth with the help of the ubiquitous analyst that cheered the audience now. At that thought, Michael came immediately to mind.

Poor Michael, plunging to the depths of his unconscious thoughts to discover that he could respond more positively to an aggressive woman but be attracted to a passive, docile sort. He must, therefore, mold his lover of preference to accommodate the psyche he only intellectually comprehends. His analysis of minutiae has made every gesture, every word, a double-edged sword, worthy of deliberation and dissection.

Poor Michael—which seems to be his name now—is dedicated to straightening out his "screwed-up" life and in the meanwhile probably pontificating with unquestioned authority to another soul in search of a workable psyche. How little they know about Poor Michael's own special torment, well concealed behind the façade of an elegant office and several pieces of framed paper.

Leave Poor Michael alone, Diane chided herself. *He's desperately trying to put his life into some order he can comprehend. What has Ellen done but pout about the cruel blows fate has dealt her?*

Diane was forced to put an end to those thoughts as the bell announced Joan's arrival. The topic of discussion would be Mitchell, of course.

"Hi," they greeted each other almost at the same time.

"Mom came over and she's playing with the kids, so I thought I'd come up and get away for a while," said Joan with a sigh as she parked herself on the couch.

"What's happening?" asked Diane.

"Well, nothing terribly great. Mitchell told me that he's invited his girlfriend to share his apartment and he expects the children to adjust to the situation. I'm consulting my lawyer in a few days. I want to restrict his visits and his rights. The children, though, are getting confused and becoming more difficult to manage. It must be a passing phase. Children can be like that when they don't get their own way," she informed Diane, with a trace of doubt in her voice.

"Poor kids, they don't know what's happening," said Diane, instinctively understanding their plight as the most disabling and, unknowingly, identifying with their dilemma. "Their world is crumbling, and they dare not wonder what will be next or even what part they played in its destruction."

"You're probably right, but when I get caught up in him and them, I don't have time to work it out without becoming emotional. Besides, my shrink says it's good I'm getting in touch with my feelings."

"Joan, if I hear you refer to your 'shrink' one more time, I think I'll scream. I'm starting to attribute more insidious motives to these people than you can believe. Look at Ellen. I think she wasn't doing too badly until the analyst came into the picture. Why don't we just go into an empty, soundproof room and scream away? Lately that's what I think I'd like to do. Let it all out without it reaching anyone else's ears. Damn it all. Let's forget men for a while."

"What are you doing about dinner tonight?" asked a subdued Joan, taken aback by her friend's outburst.

"Allie's coming over. I bought some bread and cheese and wine and I have some fruit." Suddenly Diane started laughing, softly at first and then louder, less contained, almost like an hysterical reaction. Joan looked at her, puzzled at first and then concerned. Tears rolled down her cheeks, the mad sounds filled with cries and then spasms of laughter, shaking her body and renewing the cycle. The laughter finally subsided, and Diane wiped her tear-drenched eyes.

"Whatever caused that?" asked Joan incredulously.

"Well," said Diane between small episodes of laughter, "I had just finished telling you that we should stop talking about men for a while when I realized Allie was coming over, and what do you think the topic of conversation will be? Men, of course." She teared up now but wiped away the tears, blinking them back and shaking her head, as if to rid herself of the thoughts.

Joan put her arm around her and patted her. "I'm sorry," Diane said, "maybe my hands are aching me, bothering me. That's it. It's all starting to get to me," she said as she cried even harder, realizing all the while that Joan was feeling helpless and surprised. She thought how unlike this was of her, she who was usually so placid and rational, now laughing, now crying, and now doing both at the same time and sounding like an hysterical female.

"Please stop. It's going to be all right," Joan assured her.

"I'm sorry. Really I am. I don't know what got into me. I suppose getting that card from David didn't help either."

"Why? What did he say?"

"He'll be home in about two weeks. Actually, it should be about a week and a half now. It must have taken a few days for the card to arrive. I'm anxious to see him. I want him back. I want my old life back and our life together," she said as she straightened herself and wiped her eyes. "I'm all right. Just talking about these men has been getting me down. Pat was telling me about John last night, and Allie will talk about Steve tonight, and I'll talk about David," she said, smiling sardonically. "I'll talk about us getting together,"—as though just talking about it would will the act to be fulfilled.

"What if he's still living with Elizabeth?"

"I have a strange feeling that he isn't. All right, it may be wishful thinking, a straw dream, but it is possible."

"You could be right. You know, I wouldn't take Mitchell back if he crawled on his hands and knees. I can't even stand the sight of him now."

"Don't be so certain. You can't predict how you'll feel a year from now or even a month from now."

"I can," said Joan fiercely. "I want everything I can get from him and then let the devil take him. I've seen just about the ugliest side of him I ever want to see or remember. No, I'm pretty sure that whatever we had we managed to destroy in the past few weeks. I'm not going to lament it, though. As a matter of fact, the Unitarian Church had a rap session on single parents and their problems about a week ago. I went, out of sheer boredom, I guess, but I met a very nice man. He called last night. We made a date for Saturday night. I'm actually looking forward to it."

"You'd already started to date someone else, hadn't you?"

"Yes, but I wasn't terribly interested in him. I think I was doing that to get back at Mitchell. Show him that two could play the same game. But I didn't enjoy Ron's company, and I stopped seeing him. How are things going with you and Michael?"

"I don't know. I'm not really enjoying the relationship. He needs so much more than I feel able to give, but I can't break it off. We're going up to the country for the weekend. A friend of his has a house on the Hudson. It's quite beautiful there, and the family is lovely. We were there a few weeks ago. It's a bit of a haven there. "

Joan looked at her friend. Diane seemed a little more peaceful now. "I'd like to get out of the city, too, even for a day." She looked at the clock on Diane's desk and stood up. "I guess I'll go down now. I've got to start dinner. I'll see you soon." She looked at Diane with a slight smile and then turned and left.

Wonder what the smile was about, thought Diane. She heard the door close behind her and put her mind to thoughts of her next guest.

Allie came at six o'clock, bringing an enormous jug of wine. Her first sight of Diane's bandaged hands visibly disturbed her, Diane noticed, but she quickly caught herself. Allie was a nurse, and years of practical application had restrained her from any show of emotion in such situations.

"How are you managing?" she said after an awkward embrace with her sister-in-law.

"Not bad. I imagine, however, that I'm going to have a certain amount of trouble pouring from that huge jug. Are you planning on getting drunk tonight?"

"Well, I fell in love with the shape of the bottle, not to mention the gorgeous label," she said as she displayed the bottle. "I'm a real discerner of great labels. Anyway, the man swore the wine was delicate, fruity, full-bodied, happy, alcoholic … I forgot what all he said, but the clincher was … the price was right, so I could hardly refuse. I shall pour and you sit back, and we both shall drink and be merry." Allie's high spirits were exactly what Diane needed.

She took some glasses from the cupboard and Diane clumsily followed with the food. Then she went back to the kitchen for some plates and forks. Allie helped set the table and Diane started to cut the fresh loaf of French bread. "Here, let me do that," said Allie, "it's a little awkward for you." Diane let her cut the bread into several slices and then started to spread a soft cheese onto the bread when Allie remarked that the left hand seemed less injured than the right.

"I noticed the doc immobilized the thumb. How do the fingers feel? Do you have good sensation?"

"Fine. There's no problem."

"Nothing broken?"

"No, just something torn, or pulled. I don't even know, and I don't suppose it really matters. As long as they mend."

"How did all this happen?"

"I don't really remember, Allie. I was sorting some things, and I slipped. I guess I must have placed my hands in front of me to protect my body."

"That's usually the cause of a Colles' fracture."

"Allie, do you mind if we stop talking about it? I'm really tired of explaining my clumsiness to everyone." Allie was too inquisitive; Diane was afraid her medical background might highlight the inconsistencies of her story.

"How's your new apartment? What have you done with it since I last saw it?" asked Diane.

"Oh, nothing much. In fact, my little tenement has become rather confining. I may not be in it much longer."

Diane made a sound of surprise. It seemed like only a short while ago Allie was so enthused about all the changes.

"I've seen Steve several times over the last week," Allie continued. "Would you believe he misses me? I didn't think he knew I was around, except of course, in bed, and only on those rare occasions when work or some other activity hadn't completely worn him out. Anyway, he misses me and wants me back. He can't *promise* me more time, but he's going to try to make an easier schedule for himself. He's offered to take me on a vacation, just the two of us. We'll leave the kids—they're old enough for the housekeeper to watch them while we go away for a whole week. No calls, conferences, or emergencies. I guess he really wants me back because he can't even deduct this trip off his income tax." She stopped talking and took a large bite of her bread with a great slab of Gouda cheese on it. Then she took a gulp of wine and leaned back.

"I told him I'd think about it. I haven't changed my plans about school. I want to start in January. I'm pretty certain I'll be accepted. Steve hasn't objected to that." Another bite of the bread with cheese, another gulp of wine. Diane was enjoying the creamy Brie, the crusty French bread, and the rich red wine, which was beginning to relax her. The conversation wasn't at all disturbing. Allie was comfortable; no tension there, because she was calling the shots, and it was giving her confidence, which in turn was giving her an aura of complacency—or was it self-satisfaction? They were both enjoying the food, Allie reaching every now and again for a grape and slowly breaking into the juicy fruit with her teeth.

"If I return, I know it isn't going to be perfect, but then it never really was," Allie confessed. "He was always so busy, in medical school and then later when he started his internship. I kept thinking it would ease up, maybe his residency would be better, but it only got worse. I guess that's the way it's got to be and I'll just have to accept it." Allie took another bite of bread with a new cheese, this time the creamy blue, pungent and salty. The cheeses were starting to overwhelm with their scents, but the wine cleared the palate. It made Diane's mind fuzzy and free at the same time. She was relaxing, and all the issues were beginning to seem less important, receding into a pleasant haze ... into Allie's voice softly but firmly speaking.

"I have to start making a life of my own," Allie went on. The wine was not going to diminish her speech. "I can't expect either him or the children to fill my life."

Diane nodded, almost sleepily. Allie was right, she thought. She has it all figured out and it's making sense.

"Eventually the kids will be going their own way, and then there'll just be the three of us—Steve, me and medicine, if his health doesn't make him slow down before then."

"Is it really as bad as that?" asked Diane, suddenly brought into focus by the thought of her brother's health.

"It isn't very good, but it's not that bad either. He has an elevated blood pressure, he's a bit overweight, but it's not really that bad. His pressure's controlled, and he really does want to get the weight down. Some of this is my fault. Oh, not the health issues. It was me, where I put my priorities. I invested so much trivia in my marriage, in looking a certain way, in making my home meet certain standards, having our friends entertained in a specific manner. Maybe I made Steve feel he had to live up to my standards."

Another sip of the wine, some greater relaxation. Allie's thoughts more interesting now. Her voice was controlled and pleasant. Self-revelation to the piano's theme emanating from the stereo. Banalities … that was it. Allie was talking about banalities that obsessed her. What banalities? She spent days trying to achieve the perfect match between the daisy on the tablecloth and the daisy trim on the napkin. Bendel's, Bergdorf's, Saks … that's where the impossible was achieved. *Be serious now. Focus on Allie.*

"I won't go back to that anymore, but I have to admit that I might not make it on my own either, foregoing luxury standards and less," Allie said.

"I'm going to play devil's advocate for just a minute. Are you really giving the separation enough time?" A mixture of concern, curiosity, and a strange impulse prompted Diane's question.

"I don't know. I'm going to give it a few more weeks, but I don't think this separation will work. The truth is that I miss Steve. I do love him. I didn't leave him because I didn't care about him or because there was someone else. It was never anything like that. I think I hoped in the back of my mind that he would implore me to immediately return, beg my forgiveness, promise me his every waking moment. A slight exaggeration, but I did want changes."

Another fast gulp of the wine. Did Diane notice some tension? Was Allie's self-satisfaction diminishing? She continued saying that they clarified those invisible … imaginary points … the ones about begging forgiveness, promising all sorts of changes.

"No," Allie said, "he hasn't been at a loss because I've left. He has his medicine and he's busy, but he does miss me. He's willing to make some changes, so perhaps that's enough for now. I had to accept the fact that I was damn scared after my grand exit and all the gaping mouths had closed. I was lonely too. I guess that was the worst part, the plain loneliness. Everyone in our circle is married, for better or worse. A quasi-single woman sporting a new lifestyle wasn't exactly what people wanted around. Our women friends, especially, didn't want me around their husbands."

"No, I guess not," murmured Diane, though she didn't think Allie heard or cared what she said. She took a large black olive from between the golden cheese, then pulled another slice of bread to her plate, ready to cover it with some salsa she had opened. Allie had finished her drink and was filling the glass again.

"All my friendships with that circle were superficial, anyway. It was the annual hospital dance at the Waldorf, a dinner now and then in honor of this or that cause or man, and the formal dinners in private homes. Most of the wives were as dissatisfied as I was, but the money could assuage a great deal. You'd be surprised how we manage to submerge our disaffection with our lives. Most of us came from upward-striving, middle-class homes. The money that starts coming in isn't something one easily rejects. You buy a lovely co-op on Park or Madison and redo it. Then a little later you start picking a summer home. You start meeting people you might not get to know otherwise. Everyone wants a doctor or two in the group."

This time it almost seemed to Diane that Allie took a swig from the fragile wine glass. She paused and bit off some bread and looked pensively around the apartment, as though she were seeing all sorts of possibilities.

"I was a long way from nursing school or the wards," she mused. "I wasn't the handmaiden of every doctor passing the corridor; I was the exclusive property of one doctor. But then, with time and trivia on my hands, I started to think nursing was better than what I had. When that began to happen, I knew things between Steve and me were bad."

"But you didn't like nursing, did you?" interjected Diane.

"In retrospect, I hated it. While I practiced, I was merely dissatisfied. The demands seemed unreasonable and the job was limiting. I liked scrub nursing, the OR was exciting, but there, too, I felt cheated. You know, like a robot carrying out orders. When I saw shoddy work or really bad judgment, it burned me. I'd think, 'Why, I could do better than that fool with my eyes blindfolded!' I stayed silent, of course. It wasn't my place to speak up, and the knife wasn't in my hands. The doctor could explain the death or the complications and forget it, but I grew harder and meaner. I was just never satisfied."

Allie spoke clearly, almost coldly. Diane was amazed by the amount of wine she had drunk while remaining sober and rational. It was another side of Allie she never knew, the introspective, deeper soul that was hidden in elegant niceties and warm, conventional manners.

She continued, "You know, I've always thought of myself as brighter than Steve. No, not always, but only recently, when I've really stopped to listen to him or watch him. He lives in his secure, narrow world. He's memorized anatomy, a few case histories, and a spattering of other matters. He'll never be an innovator, he'll never question. A good memory helped him through medical school. His diagnostic skills were always doubtful, the complexities of any situation too cumbersome for him to ponder."

Diane was growing a bit uncomfortable. Steve and she were no longer as close as they were when they were children, but she still loved him, still remembered the brother who sometimes shielded her from life's hardships, from the parents who couldn't understand the delicate and sensitive child she had always been. He had been her rock, and though the years had emotionally separated them, her memories were still warm and loving. She didn't like hearing him trivialized like this. But Allie was not to be stopped. She was on a roll, and it didn't matter that she was revealing more than she might like, when a later time might make her regret her words.

"He loves surgery," she went on, not really talking to Diane anymore. "He's got his diagnosis, he goes in and out and hopes for the best," she said with a wave of her hand. Then she took another sip of her wine. A little quieter she said, "He's not a bad surgeon. He'll never be great, but he's far more than adequate. I often admired his work, and he dealt honestly with his patients. I like that. Maybe there's a lot that I like, but we never had much time to find out. I know I love him, but that didn't seem adequate compensation for his constant absence.

"Anyway," she continued, seeming to come to the end of the testimony, the confession, or just a cleansing of her heart, "I have to face the fact now that I really didn't think, and now, don't think, I could make it on my own. Besides, it will be good for the kids. So perhaps a compromise of sorts is better than a total rejection of everything I'm used to. I can't deny I like the luxuries, but maybe now I'll put them in perspective."

"When do you think you'll go back, if you do?"

"I told Steve I want to think about it a while longer, but that was just pride. I couldn't come running home because he snapped his fingers. I guess I'll give it a few more weeks—or maybe just one or two," she said with a quiet sigh of sadness.

"Don't you miss the kids, Allie?"

"Terribly. But it's been a lesson of sorts. This may sound funny to you, but the kids really have very complete lives of their own. They're in school most of the day. Stephanie has ballet lessons and piano lessons, and when she isn't busy with a lesson, she has a friend over or goes to visit a friend. They're both old enough to travel alone, at least by bus or taxi, and they're busy with things that interest teenagers. Another few years and they'll both be in college."

"Yes, I guess that's true," said Diane, moving restlessly in her chair.

Allie got up and started putting some food into the fridge and some plates in the sink.

"They're busy, wealthy children, insulated to a certain degree. They weren't as shattered by my absence as they might have been," she said, moving around the kitchen slowly and methodically. "Steve and I were very civilized when I left. It was all … just so civilized. Where should I put the olives?"

"Oh, the jar's in the fridge."

"I saw the kids several times; they had dinner with me. They missed me," Allie said as she walked back to the table. "Billy would act very nonchalant, but Stephanie would tear up when I left them at our … their apartment. That part bothered me. But when the week started, they were too busy to dwell on their missing mother." She sat down and drummed her fingers on the table.

"Do you feel sorry now about leaving?"

"I'm not sorry about what I did. I might have wished that I had the strength and courage to work it out a little longer, or try a little harder, but in another sense I think it's better that I face what I'm feeling now and allow for the fact that this wanting to be back in the marriage may intensify. Maybe I'm too old to start playing the games I should have played earlier. I don't know. Perhaps there'll be subtle changes, and these might have to satisfy me; or maybe I'll have to build my life with Steve but be more independent, do more things alone and start enjoying that. Anyway, at least I gave it a try. I have to think that something good did come out of it."

"Then you can't regret it."

"No … Diane, I've talked far too long. I appreciate your listening, but now I want to hear about you. Tell me what's happening with you and your job."

"Oh, I'm not really liking it too much. In fact, I hate it. If I weren't saddled with this apartment and bills that seem to pile up with regularity, I'd quit and look for something else. I've thought of subletting the apartment, selling some jewelry, or getting another job, but that said, I do love it here. It would be difficult to take a step down now. I suppose I should have rented a small efficiency, but this looked so lovely, like compensation for the breakup of the other apartment—or my life."

"Well, it certainly is a lovely place. Not like my dingy room."

"Allie, do you think if you had been in another place, you might have waited a while before changing your mind?"

"I doubt it. At least, I hate to think that externals would derail me. At first, I loved the apartment. In a way, I still do. It's not as dingy as I make it sound, but it isn't as lush as this. No, I quite liked fixing it up and buying inexpensive doodads my former decorator would deplore. I liked the place; it was the loneliness that troubled me. I think I would have felt that way in a magnificent palace. What about you? Are you happy here?"

"No. I miss David. I'm afraid I can't really live without him."

"What are you going to do?"

"I'm going to tell him that. He'll be home in about a week and a half. I'm going to ask him to return to me, and I'm going to pray that he does. We came together once, you remember, before the divorce. David said he couldn't live without me. Of course, I was pleased that we were back together again, but I hadn't realized how much I had missed him. The separation wasn't frightening for me. I enjoyed it at first. We'd married so young; I never really had any life of my own. I always lived with my parents and then David. This separation in some respects paralleled yours, only the reasons were so different." She smiled sadly. "I guess it really wasn't much like your separation. I moved into a lavish apartment. David and I never lived very grandly, nor did we have the wherewithal to do so. I decided to be daring. You know, you only live once, et cetera, et cetera. My freedom would be an exciting adventure. Well ... I couldn't handle men, strangers terrified me, and by the time the divorce was final, I had made a complete about-face in terms of David, divorce, and freedom. I feel as though my eyes have been opened. Maybe it was the accident. I felt so helpless. It was the first time I was sick and David wasn't there." She murmured slowly, "I think that was the loneliest feeling I have ever known."

Allie countered, almost shouting, "Why didn't you call somebody? Me or Steve? I could understand you not wanting the folks to know, but surely we could have helped."

"I didn't want to talk to anyone or see anyone. A friend called—someone who lives in the building. I told her what happened. We had dinner together, and she's been very considerate. She's offered to get me food, but I have everything I need. And just before you came, I went out myself and bought the cheeses and stuff."

"The Brie is delicious," said Allie, eying it.

The gold center of the cheese was running out of its powdery white casing. Diane pulled some crisp bread off the long roll still on the table, took a napkin for a plate, and began to spread the cheese. Allie refilled her glass with wine and then helped herself to some more grapes. Diane's attempt to spread the cheese was hampered by the length of the knife.

"Diane, would you like me to do that?"

"No, thanks. I'm becoming an expert at maneuvering these arms. See? The only thing I won't do is pick up the wine glass with one hand. That's being a little too cocky," she said with a laugh.

She bit into the crusty French bread and chewed without talking for several minutes. Allie slowly sipped her wine.

"Diane, what are you going to do if you talk to David and he doesn't want to come back to you? What if he likes his life the way it is?"

"He can't like the life he's got," Diane countered. "It has no substance. It's vapid, the way mine is. We belong together. He knows that, and I know that. I admit it took time to discover. Well, look at your situation." Her voice was rising in excitement. "You need each other. Isn't that a part of love—the needing, I mean?"

"Oh, Diane, I hope it works out for you, but if it doesn't … I don't want to see you hurt. How are things going with you and Michael?"

"*I mustn't tell her about his problem. I mustn't tell anyone. I'll stop seeing him after this weekend. David will be home shortly after.*

"Fine, fine, everything's going fine … No, things aren't really so fine," she said, shaking her head as though that made her statement definitive. "I'm afraid Michael and I aren't very suited to each other. I think he needs a more aggressive woman, someone with more experience, perhaps. I don't know. We really didn't make it very well."

"How do you mean? You seemed to get on so well."

"He makes a wonderful friend, really, but something's missing. Don't ask me to explain it ... I can't. We're just mismatched."

"You've gone out with other men. Wasn't there anyone that interested you, more than in a passing way?"

"I guess not. I compared them all to David, and they flunked the test. Most of them were really very nice, but after a short while, my sour disposition would put them off. I didn't blame them one bit. After a couple of dates, if it even got that far, we were mutually relieved to be rid of each other."

"Couldn't that be your imagination?"

"No, I don't think so. I never heard from them again, so I could consider my overall impression confirmed. I really didn't care, Allie. I couldn't bear to think of a stranger touching ... I was too used to David. Once, only once, I thought of someone else and that ..." Her voice trailed off as she remembered Mark, the romance that flourished in her dreams but never really saw reality.

"What?"

"It was a long time ago. Anyway, it was an idle thought."

"Were you married then?"

"Yes."

"Do you think about him now?"

"No. I can't even remember why I thought about him then ... what quality made him seem important enough for me to hurt David."

"You won't agree with me, but your fantasy with your friend might have served you well if you had indulged yourself." As Diane's eyes widened in shock at the suggestion, Allie continued.

"Wait," Allie said, putting up her hand as if to stop Diane's protestation. "As it stands now, you broke your marriage up anyway. It couldn't have harmed your marriage if you had had an affair—oh, how

I hate that word—all right, had sex with this man. If your marriage was strong, he wouldn't have broken it. Your thoughts and fantasies broke up your marriage; it wasn't an act that did it. Do you think your love for David would have diminished if you slept with another man?"

Diane's voice rose in reply. "Of course it might have. I might have wanted to … I don't know … wanted to live with Mark, share his life, become a part of his life … I don't know," she said, her voice trailing off.

"But you had too much to share with David, too many years that had already gone into your marriage. You were ideal together, in a sense, although an outsider can't see beneath the surface of a marriage, I grant you that."

"We weren't ideal, Allie. We'd begun to become dissatisfied with each other, or more accurately, I was dissatisfied, and I started to rebel against David and his decisions. I started questioning small, everyday things we had both taken for granted. I suppose Mark was just the symbol of the problem. I was dissatisfied with myself, I had no confidence in me—none that extended beyond David—and I wanted to find something I thought I lost."

Diane looked thoughtful, and then her face lit up. "You know, a minute ago I protested, but now I have to admit that you might be right. An affair might very well have saved my marriage. Maybe it would have been a cheap ego-trip, but I would've had a bit of the freedom I thought was being denied to me.

"Allie, this is a terribly personal question and you really don't have to answer, but did you ever … did you sleep with anyone besides Steve?"

"Hmm … well, both of us have known other people, in the biblical sense. It did not, however, break up our marriage. We had our family, we were working toward a home, we'd established a pattern, and we weren't about to wreck it for the passion of the moment. Steve has his first passion, medicine, and after that anything else must be secondary. Diane, if he's operating on a patient and I call him, needing him desperately, he's not going to put down that knife and run to me. He's committed to his profession. He might like to have an affair now and then, amuse himself with someone new, but he's not ready to change his life. I know that and he knows that. I should tell you, though, the first time I discovered his little indiscretion, I was furious. Took the children and went to Mother's. Incidentally, it took a very long time to find out about this. As a doctor, he was often called away, his hours were erratic, and he answered only to himself. Naturally, it took a while to discover that all his time wasn't spent professionally. I cried, I threatened, I looked for the inadequacies in myself, and then I allowed him to convince me that it meant nothing to him and he was sorry." Her voiced dropped. "You know, I believed him then, and I believe him now. It meant nothing to him." Her voice rose to its normal tone. "He enjoyed it, I'm sure, the way one might enjoy a lovely, exotic dinner served elegantly and sparingly. In the end, I must admit, it has little to do with our marriage. The Jets or the Mets might be more of a problem than some nameless, faceless woman that couldn't possess him any longer than a gastric resection."

Now it was Diane's turn to look hard at Allie.

"I know, I haven't answered your question. Okay, here goes. I've been involved a couple of times ... with other men. My problem was that I loved Steve. And as much as Steve loved his life, I loved mine. I loved the security, the power of our money, and the leisure it afforded. Most of all, I truly loved my husband. Still do, Diane, only now I have to qualify that love. I have to face the man and not the bravado or the fantasy. I've got to accept that fact that I'll come in second, regardless of who is first, and that I've got to start building my own life, and it can't be based on the superficialities that existed before, or I should say, claimed my attention."

Diane listened, feeling betrayed by the knowledge of her brother's extramarital affairs... A sense of prudishness made this discussion seem like an invasion of his privacy, but more important was the knowledge of his casual disregard of the values she had considered sacrosanct, primarily for herself and family.

Inwardly, she cringed at Allie's description of her brother and his short-lived flings. His callousness to his wife was almost a personal affront. She loved Steve in an old, memory-laden way. Early in her childhood, he had stood as her buffer against parents too old to have much patience with their youngest and least-desired child. Steve sensed, the way children often do, his mother's subtle displeasure at Diane's unwelcome arrival. As early as Diane could remember, he assumed the role of protector and advisor. But this role lasted only a few years. He was soon off to college, then medical school, and then immersed in a family of his own and a busy medical practice.

She loved him dearly as a child, but the times or the circumstances had changed the boy into a man she didn't know or like. He was more than a bit cocky and snobbish to boot. At those times when his arrogance became more than she could bear, she would call upon those memories of childhood and produce the image of a loving brother, protective and thoughtful.

The introduction of Michael had been a thoughtful gesture on Steve's part. Something of the old friendship stirred in her when Steve asked if she'd mind if he gave a friend her number. He must have sensed how lonely and abandoned she felt without her mentioning it to him. In fact, they hardly talked about the divorce, seeing each other as rarely as they did. But he had noted her somber mien, the slower, less confident gait, the defeat that seemed to surround her like an aura of gloom.

A deep and long-hidden sense of loyalty seemed to be rising from a deadened part of her memory. The gentle brother of memory stirred again, coming to life as a laughing, athletic boy, tutoring her in her studies, teaching her to ride her new bicycle, running short races with her, her small body no match for his own wiry one, but letting her think she was able competition.

Most important were those talks they'd have when he wasn't involved in his studies or his friends, when he would visit her room or take her on long walks as though this was his greatest pleasure. He'd talk to her then, force out the words she'd swallowed in anger or fear, the words that always caught in the back of her throat, often making her appear a rather stupid and unendearing child. It wasn't hard to see the disappointment in her parents' faces. They didn't bother to conceal their lack of hope for this one. Instead, they'd hoped for an early marriage for her and would thank the Lord if she didn't shame them before that.

Steve's departure from home left her with the prescient sensation that her life and relationship with her brother had altered forever. Others would be making demands on his life, his studies would occupy a greater portion of his time, and perhaps his newer, more widened horizons wouldn't include a shy, quiet sister. This sense, or knowledge or their future relationship as siblings and friends, left her with a heavy feeling of loss.

For the most part, Diane's appraisal of Steve's new life had been accurate. His visits home were brief, usually spent studying. A year after entering medical school he met Allie, and a year later they were married. She liked Allie, and Steve still tried to make her feel special, even in front of Allie. It was no use, though; he was becoming a stranger to her.

She visited them on vacations at their New York apartment, but Steve was always so busy that she invariably spent more time with Allie than her brother. Allie was good company, easy to talk to, and understanding of Diane's reticence in conversation. She drew her out with kind words and sincere interest; Diane was always grateful for the friendship.

As the years passed and Steve became busier, Diane saw less and less of him. Two years after his marriage she met David, and a year later she, too, was married. The closeness of their youth no longer existed. Steve found David cold and arrogant; predictably, David felt the same way about Steve.

The family was unraveling venomously. She had to listen patiently to her parents' disappointments, stoically accept their criticism of various aspects of her life and their dislike of Allie, and listen to David's criticism of her parents and Steve. When they visited, David would almost always excuse himself to practice his music and then choose a loud, tempestuous work he was certain would irritate his in-laws. They never stayed very long.

Allie had even less time for them. Now and again she'd invite them for a dinner, suffer their comments, and coolly dismiss them. Diane would hear about their problems the next day. She rarely said anything; only now and then she would defend Steve, murmur that he was busy, and explain away Allie's coldness as the nature of her character, not necessarily a personal rebuff to their self-perceived warm natures. Repeating the fact that Allie's nature was a cold one seemed to satisfy them, although they couldn't help wondering why their boy had chosen this woman for a wife. After all, didn't all the neighborhood girls run after their son?

"Weren't Mom and Dad a trial to you?" asked Diane with real sympathy and a wine-loosed tongue.

"I think they're the least of it. The kids like them. I'm used to their attitude. You know, I think as I get older, they get easier to take," she said easily.

"They weren't very welcoming to you, were they?"

"I don't even think of them anymore. They're just a part of the deal," Allie said with finality.

Hmm ... never thought of them as part of a deal, but I think I understand what Allie means.

Allie interrupted Diane's thoughts as she got up and walked toward the window. Looking at the plants on the window ledge, she said, "The geraniums are going to die if you don't give them more light."

"Yes, you're right. I'm planning on getting a lamp for some of these plants. The English ivy also needs more light."

Abruptly, Allie moved away from the window and said, "I guess I'd better get going. It's getting late."

"How are you getting back?"

"I'll take a taxi. Can I get one here?"

"It's better on the corner. I'll walk you."

"There's no need, really."

"It's such a lovely evening, I'd like to get out for a while."

Allie helped Diane throw a sweater around her shoulders. The autumn evening still spoke of summer yet promised the changes of the new season.

Outside, Diane shivered, a soft gust of wind, still warmed from the day, made her tremble with a strange chill and an inward gasp of breath.

"Are you cold?" asked Allie with concern.

"No, not at all. I just got a funny feeling, you know, a sensation that seemed like an omen of sorts. Don't mind me. Nina, one of my friends at the office, is into horoscopes and Ouija boards, all sorts of nonsense. I guess it's just getting to me."

Diane didn't tell Allie she had asked Nina to bring her tarot cards and give her a reading at the office a few weeks ago. Stu was there, too; it was just supposed to be light fun. Stu and Nina, however, were too intent on the cards' "messages" to allow for Diane's attempts at humor. Nina vigorously shuffled the cards when Diane's turn came. Her eyes seemed to cloud over when she assembled them faceup on the table, but she quickly reshuffled and predicted a new lover and a job change. At the time, Diane couldn't help but wonder what Nina saw that made her hesitate, even though she had little faith in the power of Nina's cards. She wondered about Nina's face, which seemed to pale when she looked at the first hand she had apportioned on the table. Nina hesitated at the sight of the cards but then resumed her good humor and went about her predictions with increased vigor.

Tonight, however, Diane wondered again what Nina saw that made her hesitate. *She probably saw my unsuccessful attempts at dating those men before Michael. I'll have to test her when I return to the office.*

Allie signaled a cab and turned to Diane as the vehicle came close to the curb. She took Diane's body into her arms and warmly embraced her, Diane's arms awkwardly extended in front of her.

"I'll be talking to you soon. If you need anything, call me. I really mean that."

"Please don't worry. Just a few more days and these things will be off." Diane kissed Allie lightly and watched the cab join the rest of the traffic on the avenue. There was a light hum of activity. The street was almost jovially lit, the evening air unusually clear and beautiful. Loving couples dotted the streets. Diane wasn't ready to go back to the apartment yet, but the wind made her shiver so she went back inside.

Chapter 7

THE NEXT WEEK WENT BY SLOWLY. DIANE spoke to her parents but omitted any reference to her arms. She listened patiently to her mother's complaints about Allie leaving Steve and ended the conversation with a sigh of relief.

She made an appointment with the doctor to have the splints removed on Friday. She had hoped it could have been sooner, but after reviewing the emergency room report, he decided that more time would help her healing process.

She called Hal and told him that she wouldn't be in to work until next week. He was disappointed, but there was little either of them could do to change the situation.

Joan visited a few times and brought her a large grocery order. Pat invited her for dinner, as did Allie . She was reluctant to travel to Allie's apartment; any trip outside her own small neighborhood seemed like an extended journey. Diane thanked her but remained at home, contenting herself with deli-bought sandwiches.

The empty days at home were starting to strain her. There was little that interested her. The mild October days invited her outdoors, so she'd walk slowly down the side streets of her neighborhood, and then to the promenade deck near the East River, where she'd sit for an hour or two, trying to fix her mind on the crossword puzzle of the *Times*.

She'd watch the people strolling by and study their faces, their carriage and costume. Gaily painted faces became grotesque masks hiding fearful expressions. Ungainly children disguised in grown, unfamiliar bodies, made rapid and confident strides. Behind the masks of indifference, the postures of confidence, the casual ambiance, she saw only terrified actors. They had frenetically assumed roles that could obscure the panic that skimmed the surface of their consciousness, ready to rise with the slightest provocation and force them to discard the synthetic shrouds of their being. The world looked interminably bleak, the inhabitants scared, self-centered and fake. And then, suddenly, as though awakening, she could see them again, only this strange concept was gone. She was looking at people strolling along the river, at ease and smiling, and mothers laughing at small children and their antics. Despair and hope colored her day, gold or gray, with the emotion of the moment.

Mercifully, Friday finally arrived, and the hated splints were finally removed. Cautiously, she stretched her arms in front of her, then looked at the stitches on her wrists. They looked ugly, the black fiber on the reddened skin disrupting the natural line of her wrists.

"Well, how do they feel?" the doctor inquired.

"Strange," she said, still gently moving her wrists. "May I cover the stitches?"

"I'd rather you didn't. They should be exposed to the air."

"But I have a date this weekend. I can't look as though I've slit my wrists."

"Why don't you put a gauze pad over them?"

"What am I going to tell him?"

"Just say you burned your wrists in the oven. I'm sure you can make it sound plausible."

Did she imagine she heard some mockery in his tone? "I suppose so," she said softly.

"And come back in about a week," the doctor ordered. "We'll remove the stitches then."

She walked out of the office flexing her fingers and slowly moving her wrists up and down. If she flexed too far or dropped her wrist too abruptly, the stitches would twinge, and she'd anxiously look at them, afraid that she'd disturbed their place on her wrist. But her wrists were healing, and it was just a matter of time before they were back to normal.

Diane walked through the dazzling brightness of the warm October day, her uplifted thoughts egging her on to glorious plans for the future. She'd have to hurt Michael, but that couldn't be avoided. She'd try to be gentle.

David would be home in a week, and then her life could start again. They'd discuss their future together, realize their importance to each other, and start their new life together, wiser and richer for the separation they had known.

She hurried back to the apartment. She surveyed the effects of her week's disability and began sorting her discarded clothes and dirty kitchen utensils into some sort of order, to be dealt with later. Her hands were unused to the work, and she tired so easily. She rested on the sofa, and when she woke it was evening. She'd still have to get supper and pack a light bag for tomorrow.

The next morning Michael arrived looking vigorous and boyish in his crew neck sweater and scuffed moccasins. She kissed his cheek in greeting, but he grabbed her waist and lifted her off the floor, twirling her around.

"What's gotten into you this morning?" she said laughingly.

"It's a gorgeous day and I'm going to spend a gorgeous weekend with you."

He looked at her more seriously now, but she averted her eyes. Breaking up with Michael was going to be harder than she anticipated. She extricated herself from his arms and went into the kitchen. He followed.

"Did you eat breakfast?" Diane asked, still avoiding looking directly at him.

"Hours ago."

"Would you like some coffee?"

"I'd love some."

"Michael, you'll be more comfortable in the living room. Besides, I have things to do in the kitchen," she said, annoyed by his presence and high spirits.

"All right, I'm leaving. Are you packed and ready?" he asked from the doorway.

"Yes, I've just got to add some things I used this morning." *And I mustn't forget the gauze and tape.* She'd wear a long-sleeved blouse today and tomorrow, but Michael would notice the stitches in bed. Besides, what if he became amorous? This weekend would be difficult. Better take it step-by-step, she thought with a rising sense of discomfort.

She brought out a mug of coffee, Michael rising to take it.

"Aren't you having any coffee?"

"Yes, but I can only handle one mug at a time now. I burned my wrists cooking dinner a few nights ago, and they're still sore."

"How did you do that?"

"I was getting ready to pull a casserole out of the oven. I guess I wasn't looking because my wrists touched the metal grill."

"Ouch, that must have been painful."

"It was, but they're doing fine now. I just don't stress them too much. The skin is kind of raw."

"Did you have someone look at it?"

"No, there wasn't any need. It really wasn't that bad. I put some ointment on and then gauze over it. I'm doing fine."

"Do you want me to look at it?"

"No, thanks, they're okay. Everything's healing nicely. What time is Carol expecting us?"

"I told them we'd be there sometime in the afternoon. I thought we'd lunch nearby. There's a lovely little place right on the Hudson. If it's not too cold we could eat on the terrace."

"Sounds nice. Michael, would you mind getting my bag? It's in the bedroom. I just have to add some stuff."

"Sure."

In the car they didn't say very much to each other. Once out of the city, past the FDR Drive, the Bronx, and the dilapidated houses, the scene was transformed into something lovely, the multicolored trees dazzling the countryside. Diane's eyes were riveted on the road, looking at the vivid scene of trees flashing their last lights before death took their gorgeous adornments. *So beautiful and so temporary. Nothing lasts. I'm such a cynic. Get a little lighter,* she thought. *It's going to turn out okay.*

Beyond the trees were small houses, each resembling the other in a neat progression of similarity. David hated those houses, and she supposed she didn't like them either, but there was room for a child to grow and trees to tend, even if they were only fledgling shrubs some grudging developer added as an afterthought. It was the conformity of design, though, that they both hated. Perhaps later, when David earned enough from his concerts, they might buy a small cottage in Maine. David loved it there, and six weeks out of every summer they would participate in one of the local music festivals. Away from the city, they would walk for hours along the wooded paths, stopping occasionally to refresh themselves with food they had brought along.

"Are you hungry yet, Diane?" asked Michael, interrupting her thoughts.

"Hmm, I'm sorry, what did you say, Michael?"

"Are you hungry yet?"

"No. Are you?"

"I'm starting to feel a little hungry. We'll soon be at that place I told you about; it's only an hour away from Carol's."

"All right, let's stop then. Oh, Michael, I forgot to get them something. I've been preoccupied lately. It just slipped my mind."

"We can stop and get some flowers if you like."

"No, that really won't do. Why don't we stop at some antique shop? Maybe I can pick up a small piece of china or a bud vase."

They stopped at the inn Michael had talked of, and she had to admit it was appealing, in a rustic way. The mild weather enabled them to sit on the flagstone terrace, amidst the large trees circling and shading them as they faced the river and the mountains. There were only a few people lunching there, and yet, in spite of the charm of the place, it seemed lonely in its beauty. Now and again a wind would rustle the leaves and some would fall with crackling sounds onto the stone.

They sat quietly, saying little to each other. Diane's mind was on David's imminent return and how she would tell Michael of her plans.

Smiling to herself, she thought how much David would like this place. She would bring him here some time, but in the summer. The warmth of that season would make this place so alive, as would his voracious appetite and booming laugh. She thought the scene she was constructing in her mind could only fill her with enthusiasm, instead of making her wish she and Michael were finished with their food and gone from this place. The terrace, sure to be bright and colorful in the summer, now seemed deserted and ready to cloak itself in the gloom of a dark winter. *Is it my mood that's darkening this whole day or my disconnect with Michael?* she wondered. *I've got to shake this off.*

"How do you like it here?" asked Michael, confident of her approval.

"It's lovely, quiet and pleasant."

"I knew you'd like it. You know, sometimes I think about leaving the city and setting up a practice in this area. In fact, I've seriously inquired about renting an office. I could start slowly at first, say, one or two days a week and then increase it. I'd like to buy a house here. I like the country. I don't seem to feel quite as pressured here."

"I think you'd like it too. Your plan of a day or two sounds good. It would be a bit of a trip at first, but I suppose you'd get used to it. You would know in about six months how the practice would go, how you would like a bunch of bored suburban housewives to treat. That's probably all you'd get around here. Most likely the husbands would be too busy commuting to have much time for therapy."

"You're probably right, but you forget that I'm a child psychiatrist."

"Forgive me. I'm sure you'll have plenty of work here. The bored mother and the rarely seen commuting father should produce a fairly constant flow of little misfits. And you can't forget the offspring of divorced parents. Michael, your work is cut out for you."

"You almost sound like you're making fun of me."

"That's because you're paranoid," she said with a teasing smile. The look on his face, however, immediately made her sorry she had said that. He seemed taken aback by the words and the flippant manner in which she issued them.

"I'm just kidding, Michael. Don't take it so seriously."

"I guess I don't expect responses of that sort from you."

"You have my word—no more jokes."

"Well, I don't mean to inhibit your sense of humor, but I don't feel I should necessarily be the butt of it either."

"Michael, I made a harmless remark. It wasn't meant to be taken seriously or dissected for Freudian slips. I'm sorry. Can we just forget it? It really doesn't rate all the time we're giving it."

"I hardly think that, particularly if the remark had been directed at you. What would your response have been, I wonder."

"Michael, please. I'm sorry."

"Let's forget it," he mumbled, obviously intending to recall the incident at a later date after mulling it over privately.

"We still have to buy a gift for them. Perhaps you could ask the waiter where we could find a store or an antique shop somewhere around here."

Michael signaled the waiter and asked for the check. Upon inquiry, they discovered that the town was about a mile away, and they could find an antique shop as well as a gift store nearby.

"That'll be perfect," Diane said. "I could always settle for some guest towels. In fact, why don't I just do that? I don't know if I feel like perusing an antique shop now."

"Why? Just a short while ago you were enthused about it."

"I don't know. I don't feel like doing that now. I do have the right to change my mind, don't I—without injury to any innocent parties?"

"What is that supposed to mean?"

"Nothing, Michael. Absolutely nothing." Diane's usually low-keyed and even-toned voice was starting to rise in annoyance.

"I don't know what's bothering you today, Michael, but it's starting to bother me too. I'm sorry I made what I considered a harmless remark. I can't say I'm sorry for anything I just said, so tell me what's bothering you and then let's just forget it. The day's too beautiful for all this bickering. Besides, I really don't have the energy for it."

Michael remained silent. He stared at her as though seeing her for the first time and then abruptly looked away. He took the check, glanced at the sum, and groped in his wallet for the appropriate card. The waiter took the check and card and returned quickly. Michael signed the check, took a copy for his records, and returned his card to his wallet. Wordlessly, he rose out of his chair and Diane followed, wondering how the pleasant day had managed to become so sour and dismal. Almost meekly she followed him to the car, still silent as he unlocked the door. They settled into their seats, and he drove out of the lot.

"The waiter said that we turn at the second light. We'd better keep our eyes open; country lights are so far from one another," Diane said.

"Yes, I'll remember," he replied, a more formal tone entering his voice.

They drove the next mile in silence, coming at last to a wide, store-lined street. Michael parked the car and they walked down the street, looking for the gift shop. There were a few small branches of Fifth Avenue stores and a boutique or two. A colonial-looking shop dispensed drug items and ice cream cones, and nearby was a small store for baby clothing. A gift shop was next to that store.

She walked in, the Dutch door still partially screened. She browsed through the store, Michael taciturn and morose but dogging her footsteps with determination. She saw a packaged set of hand towels and turned to ask Michael for his opinion.

"Do you like them?"

"They're nice. I just thought you wanted something a little different, more personal."

"No, Michael, this is fine, if you like it."

She was straining to keep her voice even. Michael's continual distortion of her words was beginning to chafe.

She paid the saleswoman for the towels and asked her to gift wrap them. Then she strolled around the store again, stopping to look more closely at every item, hoping Michael would leave her alone if she looked deeply interested in them. She lingered at linens and accessories, examining each item as though it would be the purchase of the day.

The package was wrapped in a short time, though it seemed like forever to her. They left the store as wordlessly as they had entered. The ride up to the house was quiet, Michael's ill humor a deterrent to further conversation.

As Michael drove into John and Carol's garage, a large English sheepdog ran out to meet them. Not far behind was John, followed by Carol holding the baby, and another child walking beside her. They exchanged greetings, and then Diane walked into the house with Carol, all the while admiring the year-old child in Carol's arms.

"John and I were hoping you'd come earlier," Carol said. "We thought you might like to play some tennis."

"I'm afraid I can't. I burned my hands a few days ago, so I'd have a little trouble with the racket."

"How did that happen?"

Inwardly groaning, Diane told her story again, wishing she hadn't even mentioned the incident. They might have seen the bandages, though, and then asked. It would have been more awkward, and Michael might even have begun to wonder. She started to wish she'd stayed home, the weekend had started so badly. Somehow she'd manage, though, because she did like John and Carol, whom she had met only a couple of times before but liked very much. They were unashamedly still in love and made her feel good to be with them; and besides, the country atmosphere was a pleasant change from her usual urban environment.

The day went better than she had expected. In the evening they drove to a small restaurant, comfortably warmed by a vigorously crackling fireplace. The glass doors that led to a small terrace were closed off, but strategically hidden lamps highlighted the colorful foliage.

The snug and fire-lit atmosphere, the friendly conversation, and the wine and hearty fare helped dissipate the hostility building throughout the day between her and Michael. They went back to the house, tired but more at peace with each other.

At the house, they shared another drink with John and Carol and then were shown to their quarters in the rear of the old Tudor-style house. Happily, Diane noted, they would have the lower level to themselves.

The large bed looked welcoming after the long day. She slipped under the covers, bringing them to her chin, and curled up into her favorite position. Michael, emerging from the shower, seemed at once jovial and energetic, not at all inclined to sleep. He pulled her close but she resisted.

"I'm tired. I'd just rather sleep now. Please, Michael."

"You really ought to say you're ill. That would really complete the picture, wouldn't it?"

"Oh, stop. I'm tired. We've done nothing but fight today. I'm just not in the mood for … what it is I indulge you in. I doubt I could really call it lovemaking. Michael, let's just go to sleep."

"You've changed … or else I'm seeing another part of you I didn't know existed."

"Michael, maybe I shouldn't have agreed to come here with you. Perhaps that was wrong. I didn't really want to hurt you, though. David's coming home in about a week. I think we're going to get back together again … at least, I hope so."

"I see."

She could see a look of sadness replacing the anger of a minute ago. "Are you sure that this is what you want?" Michael asked in a quiet, calm voice.

"Very sure. Surer than I've ever been of anything in my life. I'm sorry, Michael." She reached out and touched his face. He brought his body closer to hers, and she held him as one would a child. In this way he fell asleep, and with little effort she extricated herself from his clasp and she, too, eventually fell asleep.

She was awakened in the morning by the sound of laughter coming from the garden in the back. The sun was streaming through the slits in the venetian blinds, the bright light indicating a late-morning hour.

She slid out of bed, careful not to wake Michael, and took her clothes into the bathroom. She showered and dressed, and when she left the bathroom, Michael was already awake, lying propped on his elbows and staring ahead.

"Hi. Did you have a good night's rest?" she asked, feeling the day might easily become a repetition of yesterday if she didn't watch her words and walk gently.

"Yes, I did, as a matter of fact. But I think we should leave after breakfast. I've some notes to catch up on, and I'd like to get back to the city."

"We can't, Michael. It wouldn't be very nice. Carol's prepared a lovely dinner for us. It would be terribly rude to just leave. Please, Michael."

I won't even see them again. They're not even my friends, so why am I trying to persuade you to stay?

"If you want to leave I suppose we must, only it doesn't seem right. Whatever you want to do, Michael."

"I guess we can stay. I just hope she isn't planning on having dinner very late."

"I imagine it will be about four. I know Carol doesn't expect us to leave too late. She knows we have the trip back to the city."

Well, at least that crisis was easy enough to handle. Hopefully, there won't be many more until after we're home, she thought, the inevitable parting scene held in abeyance.

At about four o'clock they sat down to dinner, Diane assisting Carol with preparations and John and Michael walking with the children outdoors. Diane noted with relief that Michael was contributing and responding to the conversation during dinner in his usual manner. The dinner went well.

The trip back to the city was tiresome and uncomfortable. Traffic was heavy, and it took longer than anticipated to reach her building.

They parked the car in an illegal zone, hoping the MD plates would stave off a ticket. When they reached the apartment, she took her luggage from Michael and put it in the bedroom. Emerging from the room, she asked him if he would like a drink. He looked so tired and pale and very vulnerable.

"I'd better not stay long. The car is parked in a bad place."

"Michael, please don't be angry."

"I'm not … not anymore."

"Will you call me sometimes? Just to say hello? No, that's foolish, isn't it?"

She walked over and kissed his cheek. He patted her shoulder awkwardly and left. His absence made the apartment seemed quieter than usual. She suddenly felt very lonely, almost longing to call him back and ask him to stay the night. But that was foolish, she realized. It was a weakness that could only hurt them both. She'd have to remain firm in her resolve.

She poured herself a glass of wine and put one of David's CDs on the CD player. She dropped onto the couch and pulled her feet up, resting them on the soft cushions.

Diane listened to the music with complete attention, as though David's presence was in her room and they were, in fact, together again. She could see his long, tapered fingers touching the keys with control and mastery, drawing out the sweetness of their substance with loving command.

She slipped into a sleep, the music still playing. She saw David on a huge stage, empty except for the grand piano in the center. His body seemed to be an extension of the instrument; she couldn't tell where he began and where the instrument ended. He was caressing the keyboard, all the while his head bent deeply as it moved along the board?, whispering and chanting to the keys. His foot was pumping the pedal, but slowly, urging it down with easy strength.

The auditorium was empty, though David was dressed in formal clothing. Wait—there was a lone female figure in the front of the orchestra, but the figure wasn't familiar. Diane woke, the unknown woman disturbing her.

The CD had ended and the hour was late. She'd have to wake early the next morning for work, and in all likelihood, she'd be exhausted tomorrow.

The more than week-long break from work had made her lazy. She wasn't used to rising at the command of the alarm anymore. Its sound was painful and jarring.

She dressed hastily, wanting to be in the office before Hal or the others arrived. That way she'd have time to go through some of her mail and assess her projects quietly. Later she'd be sure to be disturbed by queries about her hands and her "vacation."

Try as she would, she made it into work only twenty minutes before nine. Even that small time was helpful, though a few eager souls were already in the office.

Hal was happy to see her. He gave her a big grin, inquired about her health, and told her he would talk to her later. Stuart walked over and gave her a big bear hug, kissing her loudly on the cheek.

"I wanted to be here before you," he said. "Had this marvelous surprise I got in the flea market yesterday."

He extended his hand and produced a lovely papier-mâché box with a delicate floral pattern. "You can use it as a card box or pin box, or whatever. I don't know—it was just so lovely, I couldn't resist."

"Thank you. It *is* lovely. Shall I leave it in the office or use it at home?"

"It's definitely for the office," he said with a sly grin. "Anyway, how about lunch with me?"

"I'm sorry, Stu, not today. I'm too busy," she said, pointing to her paper-laden desk. "How about dinner tonight?" she asked, immediately feeling guilty about turning him down.

"I'd love to. We could go over to Malachy's for drinks. They have the best hors d'oeuvres in town. We can decide on a restaurant there."

She went back to her papers, wryly thinking that her time would obviously be well spent this week.

As she suspected, the week went by rapidly. Tuesday and Wednesday she worked late, and on Thursday night she went shopping with Nancy. The store was so crowded and noisy that she wished she hadn't made a new outfit a requirement for seeing David. She chose instead, at Nancy's and the saleswoman's prompting, a red lipstick, the clerk certain that Diane had found the perfect color with the ideal texture. Her newly wet and colored lips would glow with untold promises.

Outside of Bonwit's, she wiped the lipstick off, the painted, greasy feeling making her uncomfortable. Nancy smiled in defeat.

"All right, I know you want me to wear it, Nancy, but it just feels like goo. I'm sorry."

"Don't be. You know, you have your own special loveliness. Really," she said, as Diane looked at her with her face twisted in mock disbelief. "Your skin is beautiful, and I just think you're lovely any way you look. Forget the lipstick." Diane knew she meant it.

Nancy laughed and grabbed her friend's arm. "C'mon, let's have dinner."

"It better be a cheap one. I've just spent twenty-five dollars on the world's most perfect lipstick I'll probably never use. Why did I let the two of you talk me into it? Because I'm spineless. Well, David likes me that way, so maybe it's not all that terrible," she said half jokingly.

In the restaurant they ordered their dinners and asked for the wine list, eventually choosing a carafe of the house wine.

"Diane," Nancy started hesitantly, "what if all this doesn't work out the way you're planning? What will you do then?" she asked, sipping her wine slowly.

"Can't we talk about something else? I'm thinking about this tasty shrimp dish, and after that, my pecan pie topped with ice cream. I refuse to worry about David's answer. I know what I'm planning to do is right, and I know it's what he wants also."

"But just what if it isn't? What if he rejects the idea—what then, Diane?"

"Please, Nancy. Let's not talk about it. I don't even want to think about it."

Friday night she hurried home from work, hoping David would call that night. He didn't. Saturday morning she woke early after a restless night's sleep. She bustled about the apartment, cleaning everything in sight. At about eleven the telephone rang. It was Allie.

"Allie, I can't talk to you now. I want to keep the line open for David. He should be calling any minute and I can't remember if he has my cell phone number. Let me call you back," Diane said.

She waited another hour, but he still hadn't called. At about one the phone rang, and this time it was David. He asked if he could see her in the afternoon. She was pleased to detect a note of anxiety in his voice. He, too, must want to talk about their lives together. They made a date for three o'clock.

She called Allie back to tell her about David's call and listen to Allie's news.

"I'm glad you'll be seeing him. I hope it works out the way you planned," said Allie. "I've made some new plans myself. I've decided not to go back to Steve."

"I don't understand. You were so sure you'd be doing the best thing by going back. What happened?"

"Maybe it was talking to you, or maybe just listening to myself talk. I was fooling myself. If I went back, I'd easily fall into the same pattern. It didn't make me happy then; there's no reason it would make me happy now. I think you were right. I didn't give it enough time. I don't think I'll have this chance again. I've got to give it a better try. Do you think I'm doing the right thing?"

"I don't know, Allie. I can't decide for you. You've got to live your life. I can only speak for myself. I know I want to go back to David.

There's no doubt in my mind. What you said when we talked made sense. Your plans seemed to please you then. I didn't intend to dissuade you from them."

"You didn't," Allie assure her. "I saw Steve last night. We had dinner together. Maybe it was my mood, or the hour, or Steve's manner. I don't know. I just didn't want to return. I saw myself living the old life again, barely tolerating Steve's manner and accepting his plans. I'd intellectualized my acceptance of our life together, but seeing him again and wondering about it made me feel that perhaps I hadn't given myself enough time, perhaps I could adjust to being alone. I don't know, Diane. I'm confused. The only thing I know now is that if I return, that's it. I can't play at dissatisfaction every year or so. God, I wish I could go to some sage or prophet and get a yes or no answer."

"I wish I could help, but I don't know what to say."

"I know, baby. Look, I hope everything goes as you wish today. Call me if you want someone to talk to."

"Good-bye, Allie."

The call unsettled her, but she still had work to do. She inspected corners and hidden crevices for dust or dirt. She arranged the centerpiece in the living room and added fresh candles to the holders.

Then she showered and dressed, her growling stomach reminding her that she hadn't eaten very much. She grabbed an apple and sat munching while she waited for David, and then threw it in the garbage, wiping her lips for any traces of food.

She jumped when the doorbell rang, nervously adjusting her clothes as she got up to answer the bell. She pulled open the door and David stood there, smiling awkwardly, nervously handing her a large package. She took it. She wanted to embrace him but instead she clutched the package.

"Come in. Sit down. Can I get you a drink? Are you hungry? David, I'm so glad to see you. I've missed you—terribly."

"Diane, I have something to tell you." His voice was less steady than usual. He seemed unable to look her in the eye. She hugged the large package closer to her. It was like a shield, but why did she need a shield?

"Can't that wait? Tell me about South America, the tour… how you spent your time." All she really wanted to do was hold him, kiss him, inhale the mixture of the spicy scents that was David.

"Diane… I got married. Elizabeth and I… we got married in Peru. I wanted you to know before you heard it from someone else. I'm happier this way. Elizabeth is too. She's a lot like you. I hope you'll meet her someday. I think you'd like each other. I've told her how much you mean to me, how much you'll always mean to me. I hope we can remain good friends." The words seemed to rush out of him, as though he had to get them out at once, before he would have a chance to somehow retract them, or soften them, or appreciate fully how painful it was for her to hear these words. So the truth tumbled out in jabbing stabs at her heart.

She held the package, too numb to speak or move.

"Why don't you open the gift, Diane? I think you'll like it."

"Yes… David, I'm so happy for you. I'd love to meet Elizabeth sometime. Yes, we'll all get together," she said, slowly and dully.

She opened her gift. It was a brightly colored poncho of heavy, coarse wool. She held it close, like a blanket to cover her sore wretchedness. She turned her eyes down and looked at the gay colors, the brightness almost too dazzling during this moment of defeat.

"It's beautiful, David. I'll love it," she heard herself say in a thin voice.

She looked at it again, thinking that it should have been gray and black, so much more appropriate for the occasion. She stared at the poncho, too afraid to look into David's eyes and wishing he was gone, so the tears could flow without reserve. She swallowed hard and looked at his face. He was smiling, an awkward, nervous grin, almost childlike.

"Shall we have a glass of wine and celebrate?" she said softly.

"No, I can't now. I have to see my agent. Why don't we all three get together some night soon and have dinner?" he blurted.

"Yes, sure, and you'll have to meet my new friend Michael," she said, impelled by some need to make herself less forlorn, less alone. He seemed to look more intensely at her, but then he kissed her cheek and said quickly, "Let's do that soon," and was gone.

Suddenly, the apartment seemed unbearably quiet, and she felt as though she were nailed to the spot, unable to move. She couldn't even cry. She just stood there and held the poncho close. And then, as though animated by a force completely outside herself, she threw the poncho on a table and walked into the bedroom. She went to the mirror above her dresser and looked at herself. A sad face stared back, so forlorn it surprised even her. She nervously shuffled some objects on the dresser top back into place, and then abruptly walked away from the mirror. Finally the tears came. She walked, still crying, to the bed and sat there, holding her face in her hands and sobbing uncontrollably. The dream was shattered, her life was unchanged, and nothing was going to change for the better except David's life. At last there didn't seem to be any tears left. She pulled a tissue from the nightstand.

Why hadn't I seen that? Why had I been so preoccupied with David and the way I wanted it to be? she thought. *He never gave me an indication that he wanted to come back. He was really happy with Elizabeth. I think I knew that. I must have known that. He wasn't touring with Elizabeth because that was convenient or she was handy. He did love her, does love her. Whether I like it or not, David and I are over.*

She laughed mockingly to herself. *"You'll always mean a lot to me,"* he said. *But she'll share your bed, your thoughts, your victories, and I'll be that friend that will always love you.* She wanted to scream but instead shook her head as though clearing her thoughts. She went into the living room, pulled out a bottle of wine, one that they were to share together, and started to look for the corkscrew to open the bottle. She rummaged through her drawer, impatient to have a sip of the wine and maybe soften her thoughts. She found the corkscrew and opened the bottle, took a clean glass from the drain board, and poured the wine almost to the top. The color was strangely beautiful, as though she hadn't noticed before how richly red a Burgundy could be. Then she sat down on the couch, not even putting on the light, just sitting in the growing twilight and sipping her wine. It warmed her.

David looked handsome. He was almost embarrassed telling me about his marriage. Could he guess what I wanted from this meeting? I bet he could. I bet he knew just what I was feeling. It would probably be obvious to anyone. And, maybe everyone knew the truth about what I did, too... my wrists. They just didn't want to embarrass me and tell me what a sad liar I was. Ineffective too. But I know they care about me. I know they want me to be happy, whatever in the world that overused word means. But David would have been my happiness, would have been what I needed and wanted. I just can't get beyond that realization.

She sipped the wine slowly. The picture of reconciliation she had painted had never been more than a straw dream, fated never to materialize. Really, she knew that.

Gad, what had I been thinking? This is embarrassing. A few more sobs escaped her and she brushed the tears away.

I'll have to have a plan. I have to start living now. We're really over. We're not a couple anymore. He's a couple with someone else. He's not mine. I'm without him. I'm alone.

The quiet apartment seemed to confirm her thoughts. She couldn't even hear the buzz of the fridge. It was as though she were alone in the world and the darkness would come and cover her, and this aloneness would be hers for the rest of her life. She got up, put the light on, and sat down again. The light made her feel better, less alone.

I'll call Allie. She told me to call her. She'd be good to talk to now. She wanted to hear from me. What did Michael say? Call me, if you want to talk? He was so hurt when I told him about going back... wanting to go back to David. He was pretty sweet and understanding when we finally parted. At that moment I almost missed him. He's a gentle soul and I was hard on him. He's thoughtful and I was... just so concerned with myself, with having him amuse me. How little thought I gave to him, and all the time, really, now that I think about it more clearly, all he did was try to please me, even on that trip to his friends' house. He had picked that special inn, thinking I would love it. And the opera tickets he got. He doesn't even

111

like opera, but he knew I loved it so he got tickets and sat through a couple of hours of Faust, *probably bored as could be. And the tulips he brought because he knew I liked them and remembered I loved yellow ones the best.*

But I wasn't really with him. He was the filler, there for me until I could work it out, know what I wanted and couldn't have. And the sex, well, truthfully, it wasn't very satisfying. But some couples do have problems in this arena, don't they? The physical intimacy part didn't work so well for us, but part of that was that I couldn't invest in him—and, really, even consider what his needs were or maybe just relax and give him a chance—when I was concentrating so hard on going back with David. God. All wrong, all misplaced, I can see that now. I'm just going to will myself right now to believe that my love life is not going to be over, not yet. I was sleeping in a dream and it was destructive. I've wasted all this time, she thought with a new energy.

Was it the Burgundy, or was she really starting to feel better, she wondered. She got up again and walked back into the bedroom, taking the glass of wine with her. She put the wine on the bedside table next to her and dropped down on the bed. She lay there looking up into the ceiling as though she might see an answer there. The thoughts beginning to form were new, different, not the same perspective as before. Then, she turned and stared at the phone, right next to her on the table.

She could hear voices in the corridor now. People were returning from the day's outings. It was like she was coming alive again, and the noises of the city were starting to fill the apartment, pleasingly, or she was simply starting to hear them once more. She got off the bed and went into the bathroom, splashed warm water on her face, and washed her face with a fragrant soap and a soft washcloth. Then she pulled some stray hairs back into place behind her ears. She pulled some makeup out of the cabinet and put on a bit of blush and light lip gloss. She looked at herself more closely, patted her hair once more, and tried a smile. *Not bad*, she thought. She walked back into the bedroom thinking that she was even starting to become hungry. The wine had done that, she reasoned.

I don't want to eat alone. Allie would eat with me. So would Joan. I don't have to be alone.

Michael would eat dinner with me, too. We could go to his favorite Italian restaurant. And, he'd be so happy just to be with me. But Michael wasn't what I wanted! she heard herself scream silently. *Stop. Now. David has gone and it's over. You don't have to marry Michael to have dinner with him, to talk to him again.* She almost smiled with the thought.

What will I tell him? It doesn't matter. He'll be happy to see me. And even if I'm not in love with him, he's a good friend, and that's what I need now. Maybe... I'm starting to see another side of Michael. He was such a good listener and I felt of sense of trust being around him. Okay, he didn't exactly thrill me, but maybe I didn't give him a chance... or maybe I was too harsh... or just maybe he shut down around me and didn't express his better qualities. Even in bed. Oh, God, I don't know. But it's not like I'm going to marry him tomorrow. I just know he's decent and smart and sweet, which all sound pretty good right now.

And with that thought, she picked up the phone, punched in the numbers she knew by heart, and waited for the answering voice at the other end.